Pool of Siloam

(The Cleansing)

By

Billy Stull

Dedicated to Mom and Dad.
Given the opportunity to drink they would not hesitate...

Contents

Foreword

In 2004 the actual Pool of Siloam was accidently discovered under the city of Jerusalem.

This is the pool that Jesus instructed the blind man to wash in after applying mud over his eyes that Jesus made from spit and dirt. The blind man's sight was restored after he did what Jesus told him to do.

I've always wondered why Jesus didn't just restore his sight immediately. He had the power and did just that on other occasions.

The Pool of Siloam means "sent' in the original language. The blind man was "sent" there. I can imagine people looking, laughing, and commenting on a blind man stumbling along with mud on his eyes and face. He couldn't see them, but he could hear them I'm sure. In spite of ridicule, adversity, and criticism, he did as he was instructed. The result was that his eyes were opened to wondrous sight – miraculous!

What was the significance of going to wash in the water of the Pool of Siloam? Pools in the area had already been known to cure health issues. Did Jesus know something about the water that we would consider supernatural? Did He/God cause the water to have the healing properties? Was it a lesson in obedience or did the combination of Jesus, His DNA, and the water have a special healing benefit in this case?

What if modern science could examine this healing water and analyze its properties? Would it have any different properties than common H2O?

People from all over the world have now come to visit the relatively – recent uncovering of the authentic Pool of Siloam. Startling phenomena are occurring to those that have been in contact with this specific water.

Maria Winston is lead scientific investigator searching for the answers to this mystery – is it science or Supernatural as was recorded in the Bible?

As you accompany Maria on her quest, you may be compelled to examine your own personal Faith and the reasons why you believe as you do.

Some valuable adjustments may become obvious.

Chapter 1

L YING ON HIS BELLY, TARU peered serendipitously over the rise. The view before him was so startling that he forgot his purpose for a moment. Taru, as a member and active scout for the savage, nomadic tribe of aggressive warriors was commonly immersed in an environment of ugliness. Traveling, fighting, living off the land and spoils of battle did not make for many things of beauty. The band didn't make grooming, bathing, or being sanitary a priority. Taru was accustomed to a vile, smelly existence.

The early light from the not- yet- risen sun created a panoramic vista of pastels as a backdrop for the silhouette of the Palm and Fig trees. They framed a crystal pool of clear water surrounded by a series of stone steps. Standing, sitting, and lying on the steps were the most beautiful people Taru had ever seen. With flawless skin, bodies, and hair, they joined with the sunrise scene to create a mesmerizing view that caused him to open and close his eyes to make sure he wasn't dreaming. The tranquil pool was the center of activity as some drank, bathed, or swam in the bluish water.

What seemed strange was the absence of anyone with flaws: no infirmities, bad posture, wrinkled skin, or anything unattractive.

What is this place? he thought. Suddenly a voice caused him to jump and turn in fear.

"Do you thirst my friend?" Two young males, dressed in white and with the flawless looks of the others Taru had been watching, were standing behind him. They had no weapons and seemed calm, relaxed, and actually friendly. Taru was frozen, not knowing what to do.

"Come with us." They beckoned him to follow them down a path to the pool. Fearful, since he had been discovered, Taru rationed that he could be killed or captured if he fled. His mind was racing with this entire never-before-experienced stimulus. He decided to follow them, get a closer look, and then formulate an escape plan.

As he descended the steps, the beautiful women and men slowly gave him signs of welcome and offered him grapes, figs, and water from golden pitchers. He sat on a low rock wall, ate, drank, and observed the surrounding area. Two of the women emerged from the pool and motioned for him to enter the pool. They held out a drying cloth and laid it next to the steps into the pool. Taru had counted the number of men and decided that he could not overpower them. His best chance was to watch for a chance to escape without alarming them or making them aware that he was scouting for a group of savage warriors. He stepped slowly into the pool. Layers of caked dirt, sweat, and grime melted off in the crystal water. The sensation was calming, soothing, and made him think of swimming with his family as a small, innocent boy.

A man with a long, flowing white beard and white robe moved close to Taru in the waist deep water. "Believe in Him who cleanses the inner soul and loves you." Taru had still not spoken, but a puzzled look crossed his face. "The one true God, Yahweh."

The man then put one hand on Taru's chest and another on the back of his neck and pushed him gently backwards into the water. Everything was so surreal, and it happened so quickly that Taru had no resistance or reaction until his face went under the water. He had a strange moment; a conflicted moment, when emotions, thoughts, forces, fear, and tranquility converged at the same time.

These beautiful, gentle people are trying to drown me! he thought. But, just as he regained his sense of reality, the man pulled him up from under the water. Taru still felt tense as if he was going to engage in a fight for his life, but the people began clapping and singing joyfully, and he felt no threat.

Suddenly, Taru went into sensory overload. He realized that he could not judge the exact amount of time that had passed. His tribe would be wondering about the lapse of time in reporting back to them. What if they approached and saw him bathing with the enemy? Taru quickly exited the pool and climbed the steps out of the Mikvah. No one tried to restrain him. He began to run into the rocky distance.

After about half an hour, Taru came upon a small cave-like indention in the hillside. Once inside, he stopped to catch his breath and get out of the sun. Reflecting on what just occurred, he felt strangely different. Taru was designated as scout, because he was not a natural warrior. He wasn't aggressive and seemed reluctant to kill. He had nightmares about the brutal and cruel things he had witnessed. Something about the people at the Mikvah had connected with him.

He noticed that a day-old gash on his leg had nearly healed and thought that was odd. Maybe the blood that had been washed off had made it look worse than it actually was, but he had no pain from it now either. He thought of the words spoken by the white bearded man in the water ...

Chapter 2

701 BCE Jerusalem

KING HEZEKIAH DIDN'T LOOK OR feel like royalty today. He had awoken at midnight, fitfully tore his clothes and spread ashes on his face and body. He had sporadic sessions of mourning in anguish. It was as if he were grieving in advance of his demise and the fall of his beloved Jerusalem into the control of the Assyrians led by Sennacherib.

The Assyrians had surrounded Jerusalem and cut off access in or out of the city. Hezekiah had done all he could to protect the city by building walls and towers surrounding the city and protecting the water supply by an ambitious engineering project. The water supply was sourced by the Virgin Spring which had its unprotected genesis outside of the city walls. He had two teams of excavators dig a tunnel 533 meters long, meeting in the middle to expedite the task as Hezekiah had heard of the Assyrians successful conquests of virtually all of the other Judean cities. He knew Sennacherib would soon attack Jerusalem. The tunnel led the precious water into the

Pool of Siloam inside the city walls. The Virgin Spring was then covered with heavy rock slabs and thus protected from use by invaders.

In addition, Hezekiah had offered to pay the Assyrians a huge payment to assuage their intentions. The inflammatory reasons were too strong to be absolved with retribution. Hezekiah had rebuked the Assyrian gods, destroyed related idols, and fostered a renewed relationship of the Judean cities with the one true God, Yahweh. The Assyrians were intent on stopping this counter-religion.

The psychological warfare had begun to take its toll on Hezekiah.

A messenger from Sennacherib was allowed to speak to a group of representatives from atop a wall surrounding the city. In a language understood by the citizens of the city, who had gathered nearby in Jerusalem, the messenger demanded submission, citing the 47 villages of Judah that they had already conquered. His stated rationale for surrender was the fact that the "one true God" had not protected or saved the other villages, nor would Jerusalem be saved. Hezekiah's representatives asked the messenger to speak only in a language understood by them, but he refused and continued the threats and inciting rhetoric even louder so that the citizens would hear and be affected by his verbal barrage. Amazingly, the citizens had no reply to the messenger and were not seemingly frightened or concerned. They had faith that "The God" would protect them.

Hezekiah, however, was nervous and stressed, but most of all he was fearful that his faith had been fractured. He worried that God would punish Jerusalem for his lapse of faith. The prophet Isaiah had sent Hezekiah a message to keep his faith in spite of any circumstances, and God would protect him and Jerusalem from its powerful enemies. In addition, God was loving and tolerant, but when pushed, He would show His wrath and power to the enemies of God's people.

Sennacherib was feeling very confident and the adrenaline from the perfect development of the siege had him almost giddy. He had to restrain himself to appear in control. Even though the conquest of the 47 Judean villages was easy – more like a training exercise – he knew that Jerusalem would be a more formidable challenge. Moreover, his confidence hinged on a special advantage that he held. More than one mercenary and unscrupulous citizen had come to him beforehand and asked to be paid for some very important information. They divulged the details of Hezekiah's tunnel from the Virgin Spring and how he had covered the spring with large stone slabs to hide it and protect it since it was outside the city walls.

Hezekiah knew that cutting off a water source to hostile forces would be to his advantage. Armed with this knowledge, Sennacherib only brought a small water supply for himself and all of his officers. Upon arrival at the outskirts of Jerusalem, he had a team immediately locate the spring and began the task of removing some of the stone slabs to access the water supply for his men and animals. His armed forces numbered nearly 200,000 so over 200,000 gallons of water was required daily.

After driving off the few guards protecting the area of the spring, a skilled crew began the work to gain access. Meanwhile, the fighting forces took positions around the city. After five days of hard work,

Sennacherib's strong men penetrated the covering of the spring. They immediately began to withdraw and distribute the water to the men and animals. The thirsty drank their fill starting with the biggest and strongest with the smallest being last to quench their thirst with the precious water.

"King Hezekiah, they have uncovered and gained access to our water supply!" King Hezekiah and Isaiah, now with him, only continued praying.

The next morning the night-quiet camp of the Assyrians became increasingly punctuated with gasps, screams, and horrific human sounds. The few servants, animal caretakers, and laborers remaining were thrown into violent psychotic episodes upon discovering the condition of the 200,000 fighting soldiers and officers.

What they saw was beyond belief. Each soldier had been transformed into a boneless creature resembling a large sea hare, ink fish, or "elysian bras liana!" They lay in gray gelatin-like lumps of smelly, vile material moving slightly like a fish out of water and slowly drying out and dying.

Sennacherib survived but returned home defeated, disgraced, and obviously shaken. He was convinced that the God of Hezekiah, Isaiah and Jerusalem was undoubtedly all powerful. Upon his return his two sons overheard him praying to the "One True God" in the temple. They murdered him on the spot.

John 5: 1-5 After this there was a feast of the Jews, and Jesus went up to Jerusalem. Now there is in Jerusalem, by the sheep gate, a pool, which is called in Hebrew, Bethesda, having five porches.

In these lay a great multitude of sick people, blind, lame, paralyzed, waiting for the moving of the water.

For an angel went down at a certain time into the pool and stirred up the water; then whoever stepped in first, after the stirring of the water, was made well of whatever disease he had.

Chapter 3

June 2004, Jerusalem

CHING! THE SHOVEL HIT SOMETHING solid as Yaniu slammed it hard into the soil in the underground sewage system. "Walla!" he exclaimed as it stung his hands.

Yaniu had been recently employed by the municipal utilities company and that day had been sent to repair a damaged sewer drain line. Yaniu probed the solid area for about fifteen minutes and came to the conclusion that the rocky obstruction appeared to be some hand-cut steps. The crew had been told that if they came upon anything that might be historical or an artifact, they should immediately report it to Eli Shukron of the Israel Antiquities Authority. Yaniu thought the paid time reporting the discovery would be preferable to digging into the rocky dirt.

Upon hearing the report, Eli Shukron and archaeologist Ronny Reich came quickly to assess the discovery. Upon their direction, the crews quickly uncovered what was obviously steps leading downward in the direction of an adjacent property which consisted of a beautiful, glorious garden and the Greek Orthodox Church, the Church of the Holy Sepulcher. This church is regarded by Orthodox Christians as the mother church of Christianity.

Shukron and Reich began to suspect that this was the actual Pool of Siloam. What they didn't realize was how this discovery would affect the course of mankind.

John 9:1-11
Now as Jesus passed by, He saw a man who was blind from birth. And his disciples asked Him, saying, "Rabbi, who sinned, this man or his parents, that he was born blind?"

Jesus answered, "Neither this man nor his parents sinned, but that the works of God should be revealed in him. I must work the works of Him who sent me while it is day; the night is coming when no one can work. As long as I am in the world, I am the light of the world."

When He had said these things, he spat on the ground and made clay with the saliva; and he anointed the eyes of the blind man with the clay. And he said to him, "Go, wash in the Pool of Siloam" (which is translated, sent). So he went and washed, and came back seeing.

Therefore the neighbors and those who previously had seen that he was blind said "Is not this he who sat and begged?"

Some said, "This is he."

Others said, "He is like Him."

He said, "I am he."

Therefore they said to him, "How were your eyes opened?"

He answered and said, "A man called Jesus made clay and anointed my eyes and said to me, Go to the Pool of Siloam and wash. So I went and washed and received sight."

Chapter 4

AFTER MORE THAN THREE MONTHS of careful excavation, it was confirmed. This accidental discovery was the actual Pool of Siloam spoken of by Jesus. Four coins dated from before the time of Jesus were discovered embedded in the plaster in one area of the pool. These four coins had the image of Alexander Jannaeus (103 BC to 76 BC) which strongly suggests that it was built during his reign as ruler- pre-Jesus. A dozen more coins were found in a corner of the Pool. All the evidence showed its authentication. This countered the previous belief that a pool that was located between the tunnel from the Virgin Spring and this new discovery was the actual Pool of Siloam. This discovery proved the previous assumption false although it had been promoted and presented for years as the Pool of Siloam.

Uncovered and revealed was a portion of the newly discovered pool which showed four sets of stairs with five steps each into the pool cavity. Much larger than the other previously–assumed-authentic pool, this grand structure measured 225 feet long. Three sides were excavated, but the full width and depth could not be determined because the majority of the pool was located beneath the adjacent garden, known as the King's Garden, which was owned by the Greek Orthodox Church.

A press release was sent out by Hershel Shawks, editor at Biblical Archeology Review. The news traveled around the world, and the find was proclaimed "the most exciting archeological discovery of the century". The Pool of Siloam that had been referred to by doubting factions as "literary license" and not a true fact, was proven to be in existence as depicted in biblical history.

However, the Greek Orthodox officials, in control of the property covering the remainder of the pool, seemed cautionary and even nervous and uncomfortable about the discovery. The decision maker, Patriarch Irenaios, would not consider the selling or leasing of the property. He wouldn't give a definitive reason why he wouldn't let this property out of his/their control. This was possibly because he had been accused of selling politically sensitive church property in the Arab section of the Old City to Israeli developers and was in trouble with the church leaders for this alleged act. In fact, it wasn't long after, he was removed by the Holy Synod of Jerusalem of the Brotherhood of the Holy Sepulcher. He wouldn't state that was the reason he was reluctant to sell the property. He did state that there was information about the Pool that he could not disclose.

The secretive Jerusalem Patriarchate is believed to be one of the richest churches in the world. It's the second largest land holder in Israel with the Israeli government being the first. Therefore, with the political turmoil, uncertainty, and absence of need, the church did not respond favorably to attempts to buy or lease the property covering the majority of the Pool of Siloam.

The publicity of the discovery propelled Israel's tourism so much that 2006, 2007, and 2008 were all record years. However, in 2009 tourism dropped 25%. In March 2009, in an attempt to reverse the downward trend, Stas Misenzhnikov was installed as the State of Israel's Minister of Tourism.

Misenzhnikov was born in Moscow and immigrated to Israel at the age of 13. He was educated at Tel Aviv University and worked his way through political offices to achieve the position of Minister of Tourism. He was a very forceful person and immediately took charge of the tourism program. In press releases and public speeches, he proclaimed: "The Holy Land – and at its center, Jerusalem – is the best tourist attraction we have; no competition." Armed with a marketing budget of 500 million shekels, he began to develop the Pool of Siloam project.

The Patriarch Theophilus was now in the coveted position at the Greek Orthodox Church of Jerusalem having replaced Patriarch Irenaios for the alleged lease of church property to large Israeli companies. Lucrative offers to lease and develop the Pool of Siloam property were presented to the church via Patriarch Theophilus, but they were declined with no explanation. Stas Misenzhnikov and other members of the Israeli government began to put pressure on the church with negative press and threats of audits, taxation, and even seizure of the property. Finally, the offer of recognizing Theophilus, who had not yet been recognized by Israel as the Patriarch, along with a substantial undisclosed remuneration and guarantees of no special audits, taxes, or seizures culminated in a deal between the Church and Israel for the acquisition of the land covering the Pool. The Church had been unwillingly forced to relinquish it. The impression was they had trepidation of the Pool being uncovered but wouldn't admit why.

This acquisition was acted upon with the full force of the Israeli government and tourism department to uncover and restore the Pool of Siloam, however, within a year of the completion of the wondrous project, some unexpected phenomenon appeared…

John 4: 5-14

5.So He came to a city at Samaria, which is called Sychar, near the plot of ground, that Jacob begave to his son Joseph.

6.Now Jacob's well was there. Jesus therefore, being wearied from His journey sat thus by the well. It was about the sixth hour.

7.A woman of Samaria came to draw water. Jesus said to her, "Give me a drink."

8.For his disciples had gone away into the city to buy food.

9.Then the woman of Samaria said to him, "How is it that you, being a Jew, ask a drink from me, a Samaritan woman?" For Jews have no dealings with Samaritans?

10.Jesus answered and said to her, "If you knew the gift of God, and who it is who says to you, "Give me a drink; you would have asked Him, and He would have given you living water."

11.The woman said to him, "Sir, you have nothing to draw with, and the well is deep. Where then do you get that living water?"

12.Are you greater than our father Jacob, who

16

gave us the well, and drank from it himself, as well as his son's and his livestock?"

13.Jesus answered and said to her, "whoever drinks of this water will thirst again."

14.But whoever drinks of the water that I shall give him will never thirst. But the water that I shall give him will become a fountain of water springing up into everlasting life."

Chapter 5

MARIA WINSTON LOVED HER JOB at I.S.S., The Institute for Scientific Studies. Her work ethic, her brilliant mind for science and math, and her narrow dedication to her field, made her promotion to Special Projects Director logical. Each day at work was – as she described it "like playing video games in real life." She loved the scientific data collecting and processing to try and understand the elements of the problems and use the understanding to present solutions or at least explanations of science-related events.

The lucrative government contract to analyze, research, and explore the phenomenon around the Pool of Siloam, which had been developed in Jerusalem by the Israeli government as a mega-tourist attraction, was her responsibility and fascinating. She had spent nearly a year on the project and was preparing to travel from the Houston headquarters of I.S.S., to Washington D.C. to answer questions from a secret Senate sub-committee and Homeland Security. Curiously, the most difficult thing for her about the trip wasn't preparing the report and anticipating the questions, but it was *"what to wear to the hearing?"*

As she tried on several of the choices from her closet and combined the shoes and accessories, she wished she had time to shop for something new. She settled for a simple black dress that complimented her tall, thin frame. *I'm just the messenger,* she said to herself. The only remaining time she had to spend, other than packing and getting some sleep, was a quick visit to her mother at the assisted living center.

Maria's mother, Elza, was born in Mexico. At age 19, she met Maria's father, Mack Winston, a wealthy oil and gas man from Houston. He arranged for her U.S. citizenship, married her, and gave her a wonderful lifestyle. Although Maria was born two years after the marriage, Elza insisted on going to college. Mack adored Elza in his own egotistical, domineering way and supplied the money, resources and time to help Elza obtain her Master's degree.

By the time Maria was a teenager, Elza had acquired a job teaching Spanish literature and poetry at a state university near Austin, Texas. The Winston's moved to a beautiful area near the university knows as the "Hill Country". Mack flew his private plane back and forth to Houston each week to run his oil and gas business. They didn't need Elza's salary at all, and, in fact, probably lost money after deducting Mack's traveling expense. But the prestige, self-esteem, and happiness afforded to Elza made it all worthwhile. Mack's "Mexican woman" had come from a meager, stressful, even desperate environment to a prestigious, admirable, and cultured position in society.

This parental bubble that encompassed Maria molded her in many ways. Both parents had brilliant minds, however, her father was arrogant, demanding, and didn't provide much emotional security. However, he was generous and provided her with educational opportunities as long as he approved of the direction.

Elza, although very loving, seemingly always thought that Maria's efforts, and therefore accomplishments, were below par. To Maria it seemed as if she could never please her mother completely. This funneled her into a pattern of study, eat, and sleep which culminated in a Master's degree in chemistry, a BS in math, and a minor in Biology. Maria felt guilt when she was having any fun; not being productive. Her attempts at relationships were awkward, uncomfortable and left her unmarried and dedicated to her career and work.

When Maria was 18, Mack was killed, leaving her and her mother with a huge struggle to regain some kind of normalcy and stability. Mack's death resulted somewhat from a combination of his alpha personality and being in the wrong place at the wrong time.

He had decided to drive a new car from Houston to their home near Austin. About 10 pm while driving a back-road shortcut, he encountered a carload of gang members on an initiation run. The gang initiation dictated that their car cruise a back road with high beams on. Any on-coming car that flashed high beams back at them, and left them on, would cause the new gang members (usually two) to shoot at the windows of the oncoming car. If the oncoming car only quickly flashed the high beams as a reminder, they would be spared. Mack's personality of being overbearing and unnecessarily forceful was the proverbial architect of his demise. His new car was found with the high beams on and bullet holes in the windshield.

Through legal maneuvers, Mack's brothers and sisters absorbed his holdings in the oil and gas company, leaving Elza and Maria with nothing more than life insurance proceeds and personal property. They did get to keep their home and cars, but they had to adjust their lifestyle significantly.

Recently Elza, who had not remarried, had been stricken with a combination of medical problems: arthritis, high blood pressure, diabetes and deterioration of some cartilage. Maria wanted to help and be close to her mother, however, Maria sometimes had to travel and work long hours on her job. She and Maria decided an assisted living center in Houston was the best situation for them.

As Maria parked her car and walked to the entrance of the living center, she wondered how to tell her mother that she was going to such a high-level national security meeting in Washington, D.C. She wanted her mother to be impressed and proud, but she was cautious not to say anything that would jeopardize Maria's high level national security clearance.

"Hi Mother, how are you today?"

After a few seconds Elza replied, "Not as good as yesterday, but I'm okay. I thought you were going to be here earlier."

"I know, I had to get packed and get ready for a business trip in the morning."

"Ok, where are you going this time?"

"Washington, D.C. for a few days. I'm meeting with some people about the Pool of Siloam project we're working on. Just budget stuff."

Elza seemed a little energized by the subject and said, "I saw on the news where they shut down the Pool of Siloam, saying it was too dangerous for the tourists right now. There have been several suicide bomber attempts, and they say that there is some question about the safety of the water there. There may be some bacteria causing people to get sick. Do you know anything about it?"

"That's true, the Israeli Government has made it a restricted area now. No one can go in, or even close to, the Pool of Siloam area. Remember when I went there a few months ago? It was very busy with tourists and pilgrims and heavily commercialized. While I was there, a suicide bomber tried to enter, but he became violently ill and passed out before he could get all the way to the crowded areas."

Elza asked, "Ill? What was making him ill?"

"I don't know; maybe the stress of thinking about not being alive and killing innocent people made him sick. He's in confinement now and being held for trial."

That little bit of forceful, opinionated rhetoric reminded Elza of Mack, and she saw echoes of her late husband in Maria.

Maria continued, "There are also internet reports of the water being supernatural in a good way. Some people are trying to sell supposedly authenticated water from the Pool as cure-alls on eBay. I heard of one jar that sold for over $100,000!"

"That's what I need! A drink of cure-all, and I will jump right out of this wheelchair and go shopping with you!" exclaimed Elza.

"Oh, Mother, I'll take you shopping when I get back, don't worry about that. But I'd better go finish getting ready and get some sleep. I'm going to see some pretty important people tomorrow, and I want to be rested. Are you going to be all right?" asked Maria.

"Sure, sure, don't worry about me. Can you call me from there?" Elza replied.

"Yes, I'll make sure, but it may be early or late when I get a chance to call. Take your meds, and I'll talk to you in a day or two."

"Ok Dear, don't forget to say your prayers." said Elza.

Driving home in a little rain, Maria did say her prayers. Then she thought about her history in regard to prayers, God, Jesus, and religious/social interaction. Her recent work on the Pool of Siloam project had made her focus intensely on her own beliefs. She knew, without a doubt that she believed in God and the teachings of his son Jesus. Her mother had taken her to Catholic Church as a child and instructed her on theological facts and ceremony. She was sprinkled as a baby and anointed with Holy Water many times growing up.

In her late teens, she started getting involved with a Baptist Church youth group, went on a mission trip to Africa, and eventually was water baptized. In recent years, she had attended a large contemporary Christian church with several Sunday morning services, lots of live contemporary music, and a charismatic pastor. It seemed to be satisfying in the "praise and worship" category and many times the weekly sermon was well thought out, well presented, though sometimes boarding on self-help principles. Maria looked forward to the Sunday morning late service and going to lunch at one of her many favorite restaurants before going to visit her mother at the Assisted Living Center. She would usually bring her mother some of her meal, which Elza enjoyed immensely.

But, Maria maintained a private, personal relationship with God in her daily life. She probably talked to

God more than any one person, as a lot of her work and time was spent alone, both at work in the labs and at home. She thought of Jesus as the Man in her life. At one point she struggled with the conflicts between the factual sciences versus Christian teachings. As her knowledge of science increased, her belief in God did as well. The science was just too amazing, too intricate, too organized, to have happened independent of a Great Creator and a Great Maintainer. She read and committed the Bible to her cerebral data bank.

The data she had compiled for the Pool of Siloam project was astonishing, somewhat overwhelming, and she wondered how the Senators and members of the committee would react to the revelations of her amazing discoveries.

She prayed that they would understand and be receptive although the information would be out of the norm and their comfort zone to say the least.

Chapter 6

311 Cannon, House Office Building

THE HALL WHERE THE HEARING was to take place was organized, as Maria had expected it to be, with a podium area on risers for people asking the questions looking down at the long table, with a few chairs behind it, for the people answering the questions. Behind the table were about sixty seats for authorized people to view the proceedings. At many hearings, these seats are open to the public, but today's hearing was closed due to national security issues.

The committee was a subcommittee of Homeland Security, titled Subcommittee on Emerging Threats, Cyber Security and Science and Technology. Chaired by Republican Representative Elise Stefanik from Brooklyn, New York, the committee had nine other members; three from California, two from New York, two from Ohio, and one each from Georgia, New Mexico, and Ted Cruz from Texas.

Maria had researched the background and history of

the members of the committee to help her be prepared for interacting with them. She hoped for a positive outcome of the hearing due to the gravity of her research and also to reinforce the five and a half million-dollar contract to her employer – I.S.S.

She noted that Peter King (ex-officio) was Irish and had graduated from Notre Dame. He was assumedly Catholic, had advocated the Irish IRA, and had made controversial statements about Michael Jackson, mosques, and Radical Islam. Of the committee's members, the racial mix was: two Hispanics, one Filipino, one Black, and one woman with a Black father and White mother, one Irish, one Italian, and three white members. The religions were Catholic, Methodist, or not stated or affiliated.

Maria found the diversity such that she couldn't focus her presentation into a collective mindset, so all she could do would be to present the facts as they presented themselves.

Maria was one-fourth of the panel. The others were, Captain Dan Meadows of the U.S. Army Special Forces, Wolfhart Koester, Professor of Religious Studies of Harvard University, and Charles N. Brown MD, MPH, Director of the Centers for Disease Control and Prevention.

There was no opening prayer which Maria assumed was because of the closed session. She knew a guest clergyman usually was invited to open with a prayer, but also knew that using the name Jesus was not allowed in the prayer. She mused that someone on the committee or panel could have said a simple prayer as the hearing was beginning.

Chairwoman Stefanik started the hearing at exactly 3:00pm. "I am calling this hearing to order. The subcommittee is meeting today to receive testimony on a possible emerging threat that is being called the Pool of Siloam Phenomena or PSP. I will begin by recognizing myself for an opening statement.

"Good afternoon and thank you to all the witnesses for appearing before us today. As you may know, this committee has oversight over nuclear detection programs, radiological threats, cyber-security, the Science and Technology directorates, and Public Health threats. Everyone on this committee takes these responsibilities very seriously to ensure the safety and security of all American people, American businesses, American infrastructures, and the American way of life ..."

As Chairwoman Stefanik continued her formal written statement, Maria's pulse and body temperature both rose. *It is going to sound ridiculous to them,* Maria thought. *They may rebuke and ridicule me. Oh Lord, help them to see as you have lead me!*

After finishing her opening statement, Chairwoman Stefanik recognized Mr. Lungren for his opening statement.

"Thank you very much, Chairwoman Stefanik, and I appreciate the bi-partisan way you have handled the subcommittee and in our informal meetings. We need to address in this Congress the many challenges and threats that are under the jurisdiction of this subcommittee. We have read the reports and frankly, I, personally, and the other members of the committee believe we have never seen or imagined anything like what has been presented to us. It is very concerning, and we want to quickly gather more data and intel from credible sources.

"The issues may comprise an emerging threat concerning public health or a public scare and panic situation if sensitive information is made public. We hope your testimony will clarify and define the issues."

After Mr. Lungren finished, Chairwoman Stefanik recognized the Chairman of the Full Committee on Homeland Security Bennie G. Thomson. Thomson presented his opening statement eloquently, and then the Chairwoman introduced the panel and asked for their opening statements of no more than five minutes each.

Maria was first and began her prepared statement. "Thank you, Madam Chairwoman Clarke, ranking member Lungren, Mr. Thomson and members of the subcommittee. As you know, our company, Institute of Scientific Studies, has worked with, and for, many government agencies for the last 18 years. We have a proven track record of credible results, based on science, mathematics, and standard methodologies. We want to maintain our reputation, credibility, and relationship with our clients. Some of the information which we have discovered through scientific procedures and analysis breaks the scientific barriers to which we are accustomed. The results are irrefutable, but stretch the boundaries of chemistry, physics, biology, and other scientific norms. We have rechecked our findings over and over and are confident in our results. We respectfully ask that you review our results with an open mind, and we acknowledge that some information will probably not be within the logic and comfort levels of many people. With that caveat at the forefront, I will give a brief history of the Pool of Siloam Project.

"In 2004, after being covered-over for centuries by the evolving city of Jerusalem, what has been authenticated as the Pool of Siloam was discovered and excavated. This is the pool which Jesus told the blind man to wash in after putting mud on his eyes. The blind man gained his sight. This original pool was an exciting discovery for both Christian believers and Israel.

"To maximize tourism, Israel obtained the Pool property and developed it into a site that would magnify and promote its historical significance. Soon thousands of Christians, Jews, Muslims, Arabs, and other religious factions were visiting the Pool of Siloam which had been commercialized in the Old City of Jerusalem. People were allowed to walk down the steps into the pool and respectfully immerse themselves usually about waist or chest high.

"Some Baptisms were performed with complete submersion. Tourists could buy jugs or jars of water from the pool to take with them as souvenirs. One enterprising company obtained the rights to bottle and sell water from the Pool of Siloam, and it was purified and sold as drinking water, and also touted as a health enhancing liquid.

"Approximately nine months after the opening of the Pool of Siloam attraction, some medical reports began to garner special attention. There are two groups of subjects. One group developed debilitating and eventually fatal symptoms. The other group experienced miraculous and unexplained healing of disease, affliction, scarring, and other skin maladies, and the regaining of hair loss.

"I.S.S. began to gather data and study in detail these two groups. We found a consistent correlation with the two groups. This common thread was a visit to the Pool of Siloam or contact with the water from the Pool of Siloam. This was a 99% confirmation with only a 2% margin of error, so in actuality, 100% of the two groups had this experience. We found no other commonalities in the two groups.

"What we did find as a constant, but differential to the two groups, was a commonality in their belief system. In all cases, the group that received the beneficial health enhancements believed that Jesus is the Son of God. In their statements, they profess belief, at least in general terms, in the teachings written in the various versions of the printed Bible.

"Now, let me remind the committee that we are a company of scientists, only gathering and interpreting empirical data. We don't prescribe to any theology or religious doctrine professionally. Having stated that, I will report our findings concerning the second group. This is the group with the adverse medical occurrences. In this group the majority were subjects whose religious belief system did not include Jesus and his Father in Heaven as God.

"They had other and varying religious doctrines. A variance in this group, however, included some subjects who claimed belief in Jesus and standard Christine doctrine, but they suffered the same symptoms as the others that were counter to the belief in Jesus. So, in summary, the second group was mainly believers in other religious structure, except it did include some who stated that they had the same beliefs as the first group. In other words, some Christian believers were affected negatively suggesting that their professed belief was not, in fact, truthful. This anomaly was noted and documented by our company. Meanwhile, we requested, and were provided by credible sources, authenticated water from the Pool of Siloam for our scientific analysis."

As she read this prepared statement, Maria glanced up at the panel. Some on the panel were making notes, some had incredulous expressions, one in particular was red-faced, and some were squirming as if they had something they wanted to say and were having trouble containing themselves. None were "multi-tasking" on smart phones.

Maria continued, "We at I.S.S. have reached scientific discovery of the properties of the water from the Pool of Siloam. These properties of the water are unique and have not been seen previously in any scientific study of record. I have with me today the results of scientific analysis of this unique water. I will present this later in the question segment of this hearing, if you like, but I will conclude my opening statements so as not to go over my five-minute allotment."

An unusual five seconds of silence preceded Chairwoman Clarke's cue. "Thank you, Ms. Winston. I know the committee looks forward to asking questions and hearing more about your work. I will now recognize Captain Dan Meadows of the U.S. Army Special Forces."

As the Captain began his thank you's and acknowledgments preceding his formal statement, Maria relaxed a little, took a couple of deep breaths and mentally reviewed the previous five minutes. She felt that she did well with her practiced delivery of the statements. She tried to formulate and categorize answers to the anticipated questions the committee members might present to her in just a short while. She tried to concentrate on her mental preparations, but quickly forgot all about them as she began to listen to the compelling testimony of the Captain.

"Our mission was to obtain some water directly from the Pool of Siloam. The Israeli government had closed off and put a restricted area around the pool. My understanding is that requests by the U.S. government for water samples had been denied. We had to be sure that the water was authentic and even if samples had been supplied, we had no way of confirming the authenticity. No one was allowed within the now heavily guarded restricted area. A privately-owned helicopter had tried to obtain some of the water by dropping a large water bucket, like the kind used in putting out wildfires, into the Pool. Within seconds, three Israeli military choppers surrounded the private helicopter and escorted it away. We aren't sure of the outcome of the incident. It was claimed to be a 'training exercise'.

"One of our tech divisions did some sonar, seismic, and infrared imaging of the subterranean area within and around the Pool of Siloam. They provided the intel which showed a large underground cavity near the pool. We assumed it to be a cave as there are many caves in the area. Obviously, this was a very politically sensitive mission, and we had to find a way to accomplish it in an extremely covert manner. Israel is one of our allies, and we didn't want to cause anything negative to happen over obtaining a few gallons of water from the Pool of Siloam.

"The directive for the mission was very clear, and we realized that it was a top priority mission. We devised a mission plan that included the following elements: there is a tunnel to the water supply known as Warren's shaft – named after the archeologist that discovered it in the 1800's. It is a system that consists of several sections totaling sixty-nine meters and it descends forty-one meters. A fourteen-meter shaft connects at its base to the Gihon Spring which feeds the Pool of Siloam. We could assess the subterranean area via this shaft and, with some widening, we could connect through a natural fissure to the cave indicated on our geographical intel.

"We would determine a connection point from the cave to the Pool of Siloam and access it with digging or small blasting caps if necessary. We, being myself and two others under my command, executed the first part of the plan without any problems. We entered Warren's shaft and located the natural fissure. The smallest and thinnest team member was able to squeeze through, and he determined that, with some effort, we could be able to traverse to the cave through the fissure.

"After about 4 hours of using our laser cutters and small explosive charges, we cut our way into the cave area. What we found was unexpected. The cave was dotted with pools of water. The water emitted a soft, bluish-white light that was bright enough so that we did not have to use our flashlights to see. Surrounding the pools of water were dense plants with large foliage of all sizes and shapes. Extremely beautiful, it seemed natural, wild, and yet organized.

"As our eyes became adjusted to the low, soft lighting, we began to see animals in the foliage, and aquatic creatures in the pools. The animals were varied in size, some cat-like, others more monkey-like, and some that I would describe as peacocks with different colors and patterns than common peacocks. We quickly took photos of the area and the animals and continued on our mission. As we moved to the area underneath the edge of the Pool of Siloam, we found a natural grid that drops of water were falling through. Each drop seemed to be individual and traveled in a maze that led to the small waterfall falling into the pool below. The resonance of the grid and the splashing water was that of multiple frequencies that were musical in nature. We climbed up and collected samples of the water before it went into the grid as it came directly from the Pool of Siloam.

"We retrieved a sample from the bottom of the grid as well, so it could be analyzed in case the movement through the grid made any alterations to the water's characteristics."

As Maria listened to the Captain's testimony, she began to feel more comfortable with her own testimony. Her information was out-of-the-scientific-norm, but the Captain's testimony was bizarre, fascinating, and backed by the military. His reputation was beyond reproach and would add credibility to their mutual testimony. Maria realized they could be ridiculed and scoffed at by anyone that had difficulty believing the unusual facts.

Captain Meadows continued, "We returned with samples from Gijon Spring which feeds Hezekiah's tunnel, which flows into the Pool of Siloam; samples from Hezekiah's tunnel, and samples from the underground Garden of Siloam and samples from the Pool of Siloam directly. We put a natural looking limestone plug in our access point at the fissure. The samples were distributed to our commanding officer. This completes my summary statement. I have authorization to answer any questions the committee members may have."

"I'm sure," Chairwoman Stefanik remarked, "that the committee will have many questions for Captain Meadows as well as Ms. Winston later in the hearing. This is fascinating testimony. I now recognize the Professor of Religious Studies at Harvard University Wolfhart Koester.

Chapter 7

WOLFHART KOESTER HAD BEEN IMPA-
TIENTLY awaiting his turn to testify. He was
50-ish, with a short, graying beard, a cross ear-
ring in his left ear, and shoulder length, black hair. His
demeanor was, as the case of some professors, a mixture
of arrogance, confidence, aloofness, and part genius, part
mentally scattered. It was as if his intellect could not be
contained in one normal sized brain but was roaming wild
and spilling over. Someone connected with the subcommittee had called him to testify, so his knowledge and
opinions were apparently valued. He opened with a syn-
opsis of his credentials and boilerplate thank you's.

"... I have read the supplied reports and have a prepared statement, but on hearing the other testimony, I am
going to vary from the prepared statement to some degree and add some spontaneous testimony based on my
background, studies, and experience.

'I do want to make a statement that there is a difference between studying and practicing religion. I am
basing my comments on studying religion. Water has
been at the center of all religions. It is the life-force, it

cleanses and purifies; it defeats thirst; it is necessary for agriculture, sustains food resources in seas, rivers, lakes, and is a magnet for the human species. World population is organized by water. Yes, the issues presented at today's hearing are not new issues. There have been rituals, ceremonies, miracles, unexplained phenomena, legends, and amazing stories of the power of water and so on.

"Many have been explained by science. Many have been simply logical and have common sense explanations. However, there are some recognized miracles that indicate that some divine or supernatural component is involved. Most are aware of the Biblical documentation of the parting of the Red Sea, Noah's Flood, the turning of water into wine by Jesus, Jesus and Peter walking on the water, and the Blind Man regaining his sight after washing at the Pool of Siloam as instructed by Jesus.

"The Pool of Siloam is our main focus and concern for today but let me make some other historically-based comments before I specifically address the issues at the forefront. One is drawn to compare the current Pool of Siloam situation to the springs at Lourdes, France. As some of you may know, Bernadette Salubrious, a fourteen-year-old girl, experienced a vision or apparition of the Virgin Mary eighteen times in 1858. Most of these were at a grotto and the vision could only be seen by Bernadette. Ever increasing crowds began to come to watch her as she became entranced and repeated what the vision was saying to her. On the ninth visit, she was told by the vision to dig into a muddy area and drink the water from the spring. Bernadette obeyed and a spring began flowing where she dug.

"The apparition also told her to eat some herbs from a nearby plant. Bernadette, who was a sickly child, soon experienced improvements to her health. The water from the spring began to be known as having healing properties. Devout people began visiting the spring, increasing each year, until now, it is the second most visited place in France, behind Paris.

"There are over 400 hotels and the revenue from the visitors is over 400 million dollars annually. Rigorous scientific and medical investigations by the Catholic Church have resulted in sixty-seven recognized miracles due to these springs. These miracles include permanent curing of major disease such as tuberculosis, multiple sclerosis, blindness, deafness, osteoarthritis, Budd-Chiari syndrome, and cancer.

"To be recognized as a miracle, the cure has to be immediate, permanent, and to occur while on the visit to Lourdes. Drinking or bathing in the water is not a requirement. Thus, the requirement to be recognized as a miracle is stringent, but sixty-seven to date have passed the criteria. However, if you look at the numbers of people that visit Lourdes each year, which is millions, and look at the recognized miracles, sixty-seven, the percentage is extremely small. Admittedly, there are hundreds or thousands of claims that are not investigated or recognized, but the percentage is still very small. If you scan and analyze the population, you'll find about the same percentage of miracles from people who have not visited Lourdes. So why are the believers seemingly receiving health benefits from visits to the Pool of Siloam? And why are the non-believers being afflicted, but some believers are being afflicted as well?

"There are two choices of explanation. One is to discover scientific and medical reasons. The other choice is to suspend our known knowledge of science and medicine and say it is occurring due to something outside those disciplines. My logical choice is to choose number one and encourage the committee to continue to look to the science and medical community for answers. But to cover all the bases, I'll quote a modern phrase that states, 'If you believe in God, no explanation is necessary. If you don't believe in God, no explanation is possible.' Due to the time limit, that concludes my opening statement, however, I have more information and would like to expand this rhetoric."

As the professor tossed out his opening statement, Maria began to squirm and get uncomfortable. She knew of St. Bernadette but had not thought to connect and consider this as a parallel situation. She also kept thinking about the glowing water in the cavern below the Pool of Siloam. Could this be a radioactive area from decaying uranium? This could cause radon gas which could be present in the water from the Pool of Siloam. The bombardment of radiation from radon gas in the water could have therapeutic effects on some people and be detrimental to others, depending on the dosage. Radon gas can't be detected from chemical analysis, but she could test with special radiation detection equipment when she returned to her lab. She thought, *Wait until I tell them about the Lithium.*

Chapter 8

NEXT TO TESTIFY WAS CHARLES N. Brown, director of the Center for Disease Control. He was somewhat of a miracle himself. His life history was full of chapters that normally would deter rising to such an important position. His mother died of Leukemia when he was thirteen. His father, an alcoholic, physically abused him so badly that he lived with his older sister. Nevertheless, "C.N." was very affable and had many good friends and was accepted by the "cool" group of guys in school. C.N. had to work at a gas station on the edge of a slow-growing town to earn enough money to help pay for the food at his sister's place, to put gas in his old car, and to buy a hamburger and Coke with the guys. Good-looking with jet-black hair, he was medium-tall, thin, and had a pearly-white smile that he saved for just the right time.

After student loans and grants helped him get into a local university, two major obstacles were placed in his path. First, he was suspended from the university after his third semester for failing grades. Secondly, his face was crushed in an accident when he ran face-first into the hip of one of the guys playing a Saturday morning game of touch football. The accident resulted in many surgeries to repair his cheek bone and eye socket. The doctors were beyond capable and C.N. recovered with his good-looks intact.

The failing grades were a result of working a twelve hour 2:00 p.m. to 2:00 a.m. shift at the gas station six days a week and playing bridge with the guys at the Student Union. The bridge games were so intense, and the peer pressure so great that C.N. chose to continue the games instead of going to class too many times. Getting suspended hurt more than getting his face crushed. The suspension taught him a valuable lesson, and he returned after a year's hiatus to the university.

This time, putting in the necessary effort, his brilliance emerged. The "Gas-station Guy" with black oil and dirt under his fingernails graduated with honors and was accepted into medical school. The experience of being in the hospital, around the medical community, and seeing first-hand the amazing results of the skilled doctors had changed the course of his life; that and Cookie.

Once he and Cookie met, C.N. had a different support system. She was all he needed, and although he maintained his friendship with the guys, he didn't spend time with them as in the past. He focused on his studies and career with Cookie working to support them. C.N. graduated from medical school – top five in his class. The guys, who had mostly graduated from the university and who had gone on to get married and work in mid-level jobs, would talk to each other about him in glowing terms. The humor was "All he needed was a Cookie." Charles, as he was called now, established and maintained a medical practice in Houston.

One other precipitous moment in his life was when Charles died. He became asthmatic and once, when he had an asthma attack, he didn't have his inhaler. By the time the ambulance arrived, he had no vital signs. The paramedics revived him on the way to the hospital. As his turn to testify drew close, he nervously touched his inhaler in his pocket as he felt his breathing grow a little shorter and more rapid. He thought, *I haven't had the time for God, but what are the mathematical odds of me even being here, randomly meeting the politicians and friends to elevate me in this position, and even just surviving. The math doesn't calculate. I have this unnatural feeling of something beyond reason. Maybe God arranged my whole life for me to be here today.*

"Members of the Committee, I too am glad to be here today. As you know, we at the CDC have a pressing agenda. The current focus is the H1N1 vaccine, Ebola, Zika and other issues which have gained much publicity. Not-so-much-in-the-news is our vigilance in protecting the American people, and indirectly the world population against biological warfare, disease as a weapon of mass destruction, and bioterrorism. Be assured that our bio-defense system is the best in the world. However, we are continually challenged with new pathogens and biological agents. The Pool of Siloam water is something we have not seen before.

"We have determined some known facts about this water. First, it seems to be unique to the Pool of Siloam. Second, it can increase its volume of the characteristic water by mixing with other water. However, the rate of conversion is not instantaneous. It is algorithmic; similar to the divide and replicate pattern of virus and bacteria. The conversion rate is approximately one gallon per day. If it was co-mingled it would transform and convert all

41

the worlds' water resources in approximately three years.

"We have looked at the data and information supplied to us by I.S.S., and we have confirmed their results. The Pool of Siloam water is different from ordinary water in these ways: it is a complex molecule of H20, Lithium, and tetrahydrocannabinol, better known as THC , the drug in marijuana. The lithium combines with the hydrogen and oxygen to form lithium hydroxide that joins together with the THC to make a biopolymer. The bipolar water molecule has a strong localized charge that can pull or repel another molecule coming close to it.

"This small cell factory then begins to produce more cells with the same characteristics when combined with ordinary H2O, replicating the lithium and the THC as required to balance the formula. One of our lab assistants pointed out that the molecular formula for lithium hydroxide is LiOH which is an anagram for the word holi spelled with an "I". We unofficially refer to it now as holi water. I say this not in a humorous context, but as something to consider from a historical perspective. That is for other researchers, but at this point in our work at the CDC, along with help from Maria Winston and I.S.S., we have these specific identifiers of the Pool of Siloam Phenom. The water appears to be the center of the bio-engine, but we have had reports which indicate that the water was not touched or ingested. We have conjecture that possibly water vapor or mist may have been the catalyst, but this has not been confirmed and is an on-going investigation. We are trying to further isolate the radical stimulus, so that we can intelligently pursue an antidote for the adversely affected.

"A secondary goal is to determine the cause of the salubrious results. Our research has determined that the unhealthy conditions which result from the syndrome are due to hypocalcemia, which is an elevated calcium level in the blood. This is caused by excessive skeletal calcium release.

"The other fatal symptom is dehydration. The water in the bodies was dissipated as one of the hydrogen atoms was displaced by the lithium hydroxide. Our bodies are approximately 70% water. Over 90% of our blood is composed of water. Basically, the subjects died of their bones disintegrating and their bodies drying up. They had a foul smell due to the release of hydrogen gas, but they were not seemingly in pain at all. We think this was due to the THC element of the virus ... errr... water.

"Therefore, to summarize, we know the composition of the radical stimulus, and we know the toxic results, but we don't know at this time, what causes the different path, positive or negative, for the disease to travel. Perhaps Ms. Winston has developed more research that we can use to understand it."

At that Maria nodded affirmatively. Sensing an opening, Wolfhard Koester raised his hand and began speaking without being recognized. "I'd like to add to the Holi water comment. There is a Hindu religious festival in India called Holi spelled with an "I", which is also known as the Festival of Colors. It's a spring festival and is celebrated by throwing colored water at each other."

Red-faced, Don Grundman, the Senator from California interceded:

"SORRY, BUT I CAN'T HELP BUT INTERRUPT YOUR INTERRUPTION!" Slightly gaining his composure, he forcibly continued, "Let me get this straight. Your professional report to us is that if people drink or are exposed to this Pool of Siloam water uh- uh- you're saying that if they are Christian or Catholic, they will be healed of health issues, but if they are not, they will die a slow, but merciful death, shortly thereafter; unless they are lying about their belief in God and Jesus, and then they will SUFFER THE SAME FATE AS THE NON-BELIEVERS? WHAT HAVE YOU PEOPLE BEEN SMOKING!? DO YOU EXPECT US TO BELIEVE THIS?"

Before he could question any further, suddenly there was a burning tar-like smell that filled the room, and immediately thereafter the sprinklers in the ceiling began to cover the room with water. Pandemonium ensued, with everyone running for the exits, covering their documents, some slipping and falling on the slick floor and some frantic with a seemingly irrational fear of getting wet. The room cleared in short order, and the meeting was abruptly ended by water from the fire safety system.

Chapter 9

ELZA SAT IN HER WHEELCHAIR in the game room at her assisted living center. She had been watching the news on Fox News, when in walked her male friend, Mr. Mosier.

Mr. Mosier was nearly 90 years old but had worked out with weights all of his life. He was amazingly muscular and had played pick-up basketball until age 85 with younger guys at the gym. He cracked a foot bone and was told by his doctor to find another way to exercise rather than playing basketball. He told the doctor "It wasn't exercise; it was fun, but okay."

He and Elza came from very different backgrounds and life paths, but they enjoyed talking together. Their different personalities interlocked in a very interesting way to both of them.

"Hi Elza! What's goin' on?" said Mr. Mosier as he noticed everyone in the room staring at Fox News.

"Well, hello, Mr. Mosier. We are all watching about the Pool of Siloam. Some people that visited the Pool before it was closed, have reported that they took some video on their visit and when they looked at it later, they say there is what looks like an apparition of a woman in and under the water. They are calling it an appearance of the Virgin Mary. It seems that now dozens of people have come forward with the same images on their videos. The news has experts analyzing the footage and then giving their opinion on what it is or what it means."

Mr. Mosier interjected, "You don't say!" Elza smiled at their private joke.

Their private joke was a result of Mr. Mosier's reminiscing of his childhood. Some months ago, he told Elza that, when he was young, there was no Television, Cell phones, or other personal entertainment –like there is in modern times. Not having really anything else to occupy their leisure hours people would interact in person- usually by going to their place or hosting some friends, relatives, neighbors or even the pastor and just talking for sometimes hours at a time. As a child Mr. Mosier would sit and listen to these discourses and listen to enough to try to learn some adult stuff between fantasizing about cowboys and Indians, spaceships, shooting guns, or other typical boy mental adventures.

As he matured he began reflecting on those times and remembered his Grandmother frequently responding with a 3-word phrase as the other people were talking.

Her usual comment "You don't say" was her very common response.

In his maturity he realized that what she was meaning by that comment was:

"What you are saying is so boring and stupid that I can't even formulate a valid commentary to respond back to you, therefore I'll just say 'You don't say' to be polite and let you know I am still awake, but that's the best I can do"

When he told her his story, Elza laughed heartily at his analysis as she had the same experience with that phrase in her life.

Hence afterward, Elza would occasionally respond to whatever he was speaking to her with ——————— — "You don't say?"

Sometimes one or the other would exercise their private joke when other people were talking.

In this silly way they were like 2nd graders that would look at each other and hide their snickers when the teacher would utter the conjunction "but".

They were close and were making the best of their situation.

Elza said "No, seriously! Something happened at the Pool of Siloam! People have video of a woman underneath the water."

The Fox News reporter on the small television proclaimed "… and some anti-Semitic groups are saying that it is all a hoax and a publicity stunt by the authorities in Israel to promote increased tourism to help their beleaguered economic conditions. Several high level Israeli officials have denied the allegations and have stated that the Israel government has started an in-depth investigation. They have contacted the Vatican to request assistance in their investigation due to their experience in investigating Miracles and in particular the Bernadette Salubrious events at Lourdes France that are well known. "

Elza said, "Earlier, they showed some of the video and the woman seemed to mouth the words 'living water'. You know that's what Jesus said, that believing in Him and his teachings would give us living water.

"My daughter, Maria, is in Washington D.C. working

with some Feds to get some money to do research and figure out what is going on for real. She called and told me that one of their meetings got interrupted when a short in the florescent light burned up and caused the fire sprinkler system to come on and start spraying in the room. They all ran out and now they're trying to reschedule the meeting, so she may be there for a couple more days."

Mr. Mosier thought for a moment and said, "They say that the water can fix ya or kill ya, right?"

"Well, there are reports of people dying after drinking the water." Elza said expectantly, anticipating that she was being set up for his response.

"Well, that's why I prefer to drink beer – no worries there!"

Elza laughed as she knew he hadn't had a beer in a decade. He continued, "But, you know, here's what is going on. God is giving 'em a serious warning. He is tired of all the persecution of His people – the Believers. Not so much the persecution, but the killing and violence, and Jihads, and threats, and evil people convincing young naïve kids to blow themselves into dog meat along with innocent women and children."

Elza wasn't smiling anymore. She knew Mr. Mosier was serious. She hadn't seen it often, but she knew he could get pretty worked up. His passion about the wrongness of the suicide bombers reminded her of Maria's similar moment of released emotion.

Mr. Mosier continued, "Those guys have said, 'We are your enemies, God. We don't believe in you, and we are going to kill your people.' They have declared war on God! It's just a matter of time before God kicks in something supernatural to protect His people. I wouldn't want to be in those guy's shoes, when God loses his patience and comes after them! They don't want to see God when He's mad!"

By now, Mr. Mosier had become so loud and forceful that everyone in the room was looking at him. Especially since the TV had gone to commercial.

"But if you believe in God, the real God, not some off-brand fake God or made-up God, or some dreamed-up God, then drink the water – the Living Water and be saved, and loved, and be one of God's children. I'd drink all I could if I had some. Wouldn't you? Aren't you sure of your faith and belief in God?" He was now preaching to the whole room. He picked up some bottled water, held it over his head, and shouted, "THIS IS THE LIVING WATER! WHO WANTS SOME??"

Chapter 10

MARIA WAS IN HER HOTEL room, talking with her Mother.

"And then the staff had to come and calm Mr. Mosier down. He was getting pretty demonstrative!"

As her Mother kept relaying Mr. Mosier's rant, Maria's cell phone beeped as another call was coming in. Maria noticed that it was from Dr. C.N. Brown, Director of the CDC.

"Mother, I have a call coming in about rescheduling the meeting that I need to take. I'll call you tomorrow with an update. Be sure and take your meds, OK? Bye!"

In actuality, she wondered what the call was about, as Dr. Brown wouldn't be the one to contact her concerning the rescheduling.

"Hello, this is Maria Winston."

"Maria! This is Dr. Brown! I need to speak with you urgently! I have a problem! I have the negative symptoms of the Pool of Siloam disorder!"

"Dr. Brown, Are you sure?"

"Yes, I'm sure! It's very important that I meet with you in an hour at the fountain in Jefferson Park. Dress casual and exit the side or back of your hotel! Make sure you're not followed. I can't tell you any more over the phone. Can you be there?"

Maria hesitated a moment. "Yes, I'll be there in an hour."

As she hung up the phone, her heart was racing as well as her thoughts.

She thought, *How could he have PS symptoms? He would have to be exposed to the PS water and be a non-believer. What is with the Cloak and Dagger tone of this meeting? What does he want from me? Am I being watched? By whom?*

Chapter 11

IN EXACTLY ONE HOUR the taxi let her off at Jefferson Park. She found Dr. Brown by the fountain dressed in a Washington Wizards T-shirt, jeans, baseball cap and sunglasses- a stark departure from his usual business attire.

He said "Thank you, Maria for coming. Please come with me."

Dr. Brown walked directly to a taxi stand and opened the door for her of the first one in line. She got in, trying not to seem rushed or alarmed, but her heart was racing.

He told the driver to just drive and he would give him directions. As they integrated into the traffic, several times Dr Brown would say "turn here" and indicate left or right. After about ten minutes he said, "Turn here and take us to Bistro Cacao". He had not said anything to Maria, and as they rode without speaking to each other, Maria sensed that it wasn't the time to talk and was anxious but silent.

Upon arrival, Dr. Brown handed the driver some cash and they exited the taxi quickly and went into the restaurant. It was a beautiful restaurant and was relatively unique in that it had seating areas that could be made private by closing curtains around them. Dr. Brown chose a table with a view of the street and asked for the curtain to be drawn around it. The waiter, who looked and spoke with the air of an Italian, provided menus after he drew the curtain. Dr. Brown quickly ordered the Sea Bass and Maria chose the Mediterranean Salad. Both ordered bottled water.

After the waiter left the area, Dr. Brown finally spoke to Maria.

"Maria, I apologize for bringing us together in such an alarming way, but there are two important areas of information that I want to divulge to you. First, but possibly not the most important, is the fact that I have the symptoms of PS disease."

Before she could ask, he began to explain. "A few weeks ago, one of our lab technicians at the CDC was testing a vial of the Pool of Siloam water. As I walked up beside her, she didn't notice I was there. She turned abruptly and I startled her. She dropped the sample of water and some splashed out as the vial hit the floor and cracked open. The water splashed onto my shoes as well as hers."

Maria, realizing the situation he was describing and the possible repercussions, began to get an alarmed look on her face. Just then the waiter appeared with the bottled water and salads. Again, after the waiter left, Dr. Brown continued.

"So, we immediately went to the decontamination room and followed procedure. She was apologizing profusely. We thought it wouldn't be problematic, but I have gradually been getting the symptoms since then. I've had a battery of tests. The tests show the advanced Hydrogen molecules and traces of the Lithium and tetrahydrocannabinol. Here is more significant data. The lab assistant shows no sign of any symptoms and in fact feels wonderful as her frequent migraines have disappeared!"

Maria finally spoke. "What are your respective belief systems regarding Jesus and God, his heavenly father?"

Dr. Brown replied, "I knew that would enter into the equation. I verified that she has been an unwavering life-long Christian as well as her family and husband. Maria, I think that you have a Catholic background, so here is my confession. I, as a Doctor and scientist have always looked for facts, data, hypothesis and conclusion, and have not seen tangible evidence of God and Jesus as His Son. So technically, I am a non-believer. I have considered myself too intelligent to believe in Faith.

I now know that is an ironic paradox. I think I now have the proof I have been searching for of the Supernatural. By that, I mean beyond science as we know it. Maria, I have asked you to meet with me about this as I respect your scientific expertise as well as your open mind beyond science as presented by you at the subcommittee hearings. I learned a lot at that meeting and want to ask for your help. This obviously is threatening to me, but there is a second issue that is threatening to us both."

Maria sat without eating, intently focused on what Dr. Brown was saying to her. The waiter reappeared with the entrees. She realized she had not eaten anything. She began to nibble on her food after the waiter gave her a puzzled look. She didn't feel like eating but didn't want to gain any attention by not eating. After the waiter left, Dr. Brown dropped the bombshell.

"Maria, you need to know that some factions that

are opposed to the belief systems that are apparently causing the positive results of the exposure to the Pool water are convinced that we, which includes the U.S. government, the CDC, and your company, I.S.S., have or are in the process of developing a weapon of mass destruction of a chemical nature. They have seen the health decline of people of their proclivity and have noted the exclusion of the negative issues with people who counter their beliefs.

There is a contained area of the Pool water, but it is growing exponentially to the degree that these countries and factions are alarmed and focusing on the phenomena. They think we are the masterminds behind this perceived weapon. We have experienced attempted hacking of our computer network and servers, an attempted break in at our main lab, and the attempted assassination of one of our top scientists at the CDC that has been the lead on the Pool of Siloam research. She is recovering, but we see the danger clearly. We've also picked up intelligence chatter which adds to the confirmation. I didn't get to reveal this at the Subcommittee meeting, but I have alerted Homeland Security and the FBI. However, I haven't disclosed my symptoms of Siloam Syndrome to anyone but you and my close medical team."

Maria was naturally stunned at what he revealed to her, however her computer-brain analyzed the data he presented, and she formulated her response.

"Dr. Brown, thank you for this critical information. I'm sure you could contact others to help, but I, 100%, believe what you have told me, and I will give you my response.

First, regarding your symptoms, on a personal level I am extremely sorry to hear of this, and I will promise to do everything I possibly can to help you; scientifically and otherwise. I have some tests in mind that I have thought of while on this trip to see if I can find a scientific explanation, but what could psychoanalyze a person's belief system and cause physical and mental change based on the results is beyond any knowledge that we have. I recognize it as Supernatural. As we used to say in my church 'It's a God Thing'.

The biblical account of Jesus says that Jesus stated that he performed miracles because that is what it takes to convince people to believe in his teachings- That He is the Son of the one and only God and was sent to us by his Father, God, He was sent to teach us and give us knowledge as to what God wants, and that whosoever believes in Him will not perish but have everlasting life. Jesus states that He is the Living Water. Dr. Brown, you have direct knowledge of this phenomena, and I think your intelligence will see this as proof of His Supernatural power. You have to succumb to Faith. There are things science cannot explain."

Dr. Brown had pushed his plate away and was listening intently.

Maria continued. "A recent statement that I saw about Faith that I related to was 'Faith is the bird that sings in the dark before the light of dawn'. Dr. Brown, you must believe with all of your heart and mind in the simple fact that Jesus is the Son of the One and Only God, wholly repent, and ask forgiveness for your sins. For this you will be saved in the afterlife and, in this case, also be saved here in this human life. Dr., assume this bottled water is Siloam Water. If you drink it, you will be saved spiritually and physically if you truly believe. If you don't have faith and believe in these things, your intake of this water will cause the negative symptoms of Siloam Syndrome."

As Maria spoke Dr., Brown's facial expression and body language softened, changing from nervous, anxious, and fearful to relaxed and comfortable as if he had just completed a therapeutic massage.

Maria continued. "Dr. Brown, may I pray with you? I have never lead anyone to Christ, but I have witnessed it at church many times. Let Faith and Belief come over you deeply as I pray?"

With tears in his eyes Dr. Brown said, "Please Maria, pray for me, and then I will pray for forgiveness."

Maria took his hand, bowed her head, closed her eyes and began to pray. She prayed with emotion, with fervor, with conviction, and genuine absence of barriers between her and God. As she prayed Dr. Brown would pray with her saying "God forgive me, I believe!" He repeated these words eight times and then became silent. Maria felt something warm on her hands. She stopped her prayer, looked up and saw Dr. Brown bleeding profusely from his throat and neck. She screamed for help...

Chapter 12

MATTHEW IRVINE HAD JUST RECEIVED his assignment. Matthew's worked as a media and photo journalist for ABC News Network. His recent work had been in Pakistan, but his new assignment was to travel to Jerusalem to cover a press conference by the government of Israel at the authenticated Pool of Siloam. The press conference intent was to address the recent investigation into the Pool of Siloam and the results of that investigation. Closing the Pool had severely hurt Israel's tourism revenue, and they wanted to give information and a scheduled date for it to re-open, obviously to help restore the tourism decline.

As Matthew packed, he received an email from his colleague, Thomas Bishop. Thomas was Matthew's counterpart at BBC World News. The message asked if Matthew was attending the Israeli press conference, and if so, would he be staying at the Hilton Hotel where they both had stayed before on another assignment.

Matthew said he would be there the Saturday before Easter. Thomas replied back, and they set a time to meet with fellow journalists, Andrew and John, at the hotel restaurant at 7:00pm Saturday evening.

The four met at the stated time and date. The two other men worked for Fox News and CNN. In the excited, but professional conversation, mention was made of some of the other photo /media journalists that they expected to be there. Included were Thaddeus Moore, Phillip Houston, James Stuart and James Hall, Bartholomew (Bart) Evans, Peter Jennings, Jr., Simon Crowell and Jude Tyler. They are all colleagues from other networks including Al Jazeera.

They cautiously began to share the rumors and conjecture about the Pool of Siloam Phenomena. Matthew shared. "The water from the Pool is considered to have powerful Supernatural spiritual healing properties. I heard of one sale on eBay of over $100,000 for a pint of the water-Certified Authentic. It was rumored that the proclaimed atheist Bill Maher was the purchaser. He is known to have major cancer." They laughed at the irony if, in fact, that was true.

They all perceived that there was some substantiation to the rumors that the Water could heal some people and be harmful to others. They heard that several governments were investigating including the United States, Israel, and possibly German scientists as well. They all agreed that they would be excited to hear what the Israeli Authorities had to say at the press conference which was scheduled at 1400 hours on Easter Sunday.

Security was tight the next day at the Pool of Siloam. Complex stages of validation were required including three stations to verify passports, invitation documents, press IDs, and x-ray of all equipment, including cell phones, recording devices and cameras.

A tent was erected beside the Pool for the members of the press and photojournalists. A platform which had a podium and seven chairs was about thirty meters away from the tent. Obviously, it was set up to get some photos and footage of the Pool to maximize the exposure and publicity.

The twelve members of the Press became focused on setting up their cameras and audio as the time neared for the event. They had been told that the speaker would be Azir Farik, the head of National Security, followed by several Israeli scientists. The address would be in English.

At exactly 1400 hours as the platform was being populated by the seven dignitaries, a bright light of unusual, to say the least, character began to emit from the center area of The Pool of Siloam. It appeared like a bright, glowing mist that radiated and shimmered. The Press turned their cameras toward the light. They captured a figure that could only be described as supernatural but having compelling attraction; a sense of overpowering love; a magnetism; an aura of dimension; a captivating beauty that encompasses sight, smell; even touch somehow; and hearing.

Then, the figure spoke, "I am The Living Water. He that believes in Me will not perish but have Infinite Life."

What was spoken was in every known language at the same time. Just as quickly as it began, it faded away. The whole sequence was exactly fifty-nine seconds. To those witnessing the event it seemed like hours or an undetermined amount of time. Israeli

Special Forces began diving into the Pool. Other Special Forces formed a wall around the seven dignitaries.

The reaction from the other journalists were generally the same as Matthew. As a veteran media journalist, he had seen, observed, and experienced innumerable dramatic situations and events. Never had he been awestruck. Witnessing and experiencing what had just occurred was a life-changing fifty-nine seconds. He felt sensations, emotions, feelings, and heightened awareness as never before or even imagined. It was like the thrill of the first time he was pushed back in the seat when the airplane took off multiplied by an incalculable number. It was on the edge of orgasmic but asexual. It was instantly addictive.

And the Aroma: the aroma itself made Matthew vow to do ANYTHING to experience it again – leave his job; forfeit his career, or travel to the ends of the Earth in search of this Sacrament. Matthew had read many sci-fi books about earthlings traveling to unknown Space Worlds and discovering never-before encountered smells. The perfume during this event and lingering afterward was an incredible sensation Matthew hadn't come close to perceiving before. He felt like he was floating, weightless, youthful; that his mind had been opened beyond physical limits. He felt any sacrifice would be worth it to be consumed again by this supernatural scent.

The reaction from all that were there was that they had witnessed a supernatural event. They had no doubt that Jesus had appeared with the message about the Living Water.

The only one skeptical was Thomas. He commented that it was an elaborate Hollywood-type hoax to drum up more tourism to Israel. Admittedly at some distance, Thomas said that he couldn't see any holes in the figure's hands or side. No one else but Thomas doubted at all. The senses of the other eleven had been stimulated beyond description.

All 12 media journalists felt a strange bond to each other...

In less than an hour the message/video was transmitted around the world.

Chapter 13

MARIA WAS BACK FROM HER trip to D.C. and back in her lab at I.S.S. She began telling her lab assistant, Anita, about her Washington D.C. experience.

"…and Dr. Brown survived his throat being cut. In fact, He healed so rapidly that he was out of the hospital and back at work at the CDC in two days! They said it was a miracle if there ever was one. His throat had been cut deeply. I've never seen such a gruesome sight!"

"What could have been behind this miracle?"

"Anita, I don't know, but we were discussing the Pool of Siloam Phenom. He had been exposed to the actual water in an accident at the CDC, and he was explaining that he had the negative symptoms. I talked to him about his core belief system. We were deep in prayer, and he was asking for forgiveness and repenting and shifting his heart to God when the attack happened right at our private table! I did get one text from him. It said 'Thank you and Thank God. Quarantined. Talk soon…'. I hear they're running tests on him at the

CDC but apparently, he's better than ever now. I'm sure he'll contact me after the quarantine is lifted"

"Maria, this is amazing! I'm so glad you weren't harmed and are back safe." Anita couldn't restrain herself and gave Maria a quick hug.

Regaining her professionalism, she said, "I've run the tests that you asked for, and I sent the data to your computer. The Siloam Water sample has been in the temperature-controlled vault and adjusted each day to the exact temperature and humidity in Jerusalem. I was able to run the tests using the small sample you assigned to me."

Starting to focus on her scientific quest, Maria said "Thanks Anita. I'm going to work here tonight. I have a lot I want to do. I'll see you in the morning"

Leaving, Anita said, "Very good! I'll see you in the morning, Maria."

Maria checked the results of the tests that she had Anita run. The suspicion of Radon Gas exposure turned out to be negative. No radiation from any source was present in the Water.

Maria knew that water has unique properties. It's a molecule comprised of Hydrogen and Oxygen with the Oxygen side having a negative charge. This polarity situation makes water cohesive with itself and other water as well as adhesive. She knew water dissolves more substances than any other solution. She thought maybe the Siloam Water had dissolved some rare or unique combination of elements or minerals, or even gas that enabled it to have incredible effects on humans. Her tests showed it was nutritious for plants —like rain water that contains Nitrogen, but it had no Nitrogen evident in her analysis.

She couldn't help but think of the Blind Man and Jesus. She wondered again, as she had many times before in her Christian journey, *Why didn't Jesus just restore the Blind Man's sight on the spot? Jesus certainly had the power and could do that. Why did Jesus instruct the Blind Man to go to the Pool of Siloam and wash off the mud/spittle mixture that Jesus made and placed over the man's eyes?* Maria had thought in years past, before the Siloam Syndrome existed, that the reason may have been symbolic of showing obedience. *Had the Pool already been known before then as having healing properties?*

Just then she got a priority news text on her phone. It contained the news about the Apparition at the Pool. Like an electric shock it occurred to her that it could be possible that that Jesus knew over 2000 years ago that the Pool of Siloam would be the Epicenter of this Spiritual Cleansing; this weeding of God's Earthly Garden; this apparent righting of Earthly spiritualization; this end of God's loving patience with the rogues, the unbelievers, the murderers, the ungodly. *Could this be why Jesus sent the Blind Man to the Pool of Siloam?*

Chapter 14

NOW, MORE THAN EVER, MARIA wanted to investigate deeper into the Water. She had an idea to try. She spent a couple of hours running tests with ultraviolet light. She knew normal water could be disinfected with exposure to enough UV light at the man-made frequency of 254 nanometers. This is a frequency not contained in the Sun's rays. Scientists discovered that specific wavelength of ultraviolet light changed the DNA of micro-organisms causing them to not be able to replicate. The pathogens would then perish.

Maria performed tests at 254 nanometers, but no change in the Pool Water was evident. Her lab was equipped with literally millions of dollars of the latest scientific test equipment and computer programs. Most labs wouldn't have the capability, but she decided to experiment with other UV wavelengths. As she scanned the sample of water nothing happened until she set the UV wave length to 127 nanometers. To her surprise the Water began to vibrate. She was startled and said "Oh Wow!" She wasn't expecting that to happen. As she increased the voltage the Water vibrated faster and took on a blueish/white glow. She repeated the test. It didn't seem scientifically plausible, but the same phenomena occurred.

By then it was very late. Maria was tired and decided to stop for the night, go home, get some sleep and think about what might be occurring with the UV and Water. In addition, when the Pool Water vibrated and glowed she felt an unusual energy depletion in her own body. This was a little unnerving. She knew that, as exciting as it may be, rest would produce better thinking, fresh perspectives, and letting the facts roll around in her sub-conscious yielded more cognitive conclusions, so she stopped her work and left to drive to her home.

As Maria was driving to her apartment, the magnitude of her potential discovery hit her hard. Her heart began beating fast and she began to sweat.

Do I have the knowledge and ability to stop what God has put in motion? What if more testing of the UV light results in an antidote to the Siloam Water? God help me, I need your divine supernatural power to guide me as to what your will requires. You are infinitely powerful and omniscient. Why would you give me the key of knowledge to change the course of the amazing consequences resulting from the effects of the Siloam Water on Mankind?

Maria had already, in a classic scientific method, developed a general prognosis of the cause and effect the Siloam Water would have as it gradually spread world-wide. There would be a cleansing of the population removing Atheists, Agnostics, and true believers of false religious doctrine. It would be a Faith –Test on Mankind. Christians, Catholics, and those professed believers, that were only doing lip-service and truly didn't believe in their "heart" or whatever organ or combination of organs such as the heart plus brain plus nervous system comprising True Faith, would suffer elimination.

As the evidence of the beneficial miracles of Siloam became evident and were confirmed over and over, the effects on society would be profound. Masses would leave other false belief systems to convert to the proven source of the miracles of healing, improved health, happiness, and myriads of other positive benefits life as well as the ultimate benefit – Afterlife in Heaven. Choose the truth or die a debilitating, smelly death. They would still have "free choice", however the wrong choice would require a heavy price. People are smart, and conversion will be massive. Most importantly was that they couldn't fake it. The psychological/spiritual analysis appears to be more accurate than a lie detector. The anatomy of the analysis was far beyond our level of science and understanding.

"What should I do, God?" Exhausted, Maria repeated this over and over in her fitful sleep…

After two hours, she woke with thoughts of her dilemma. If she lied to I.S.S. and didn't divulge this information about a way to alter the Pool Water, she could be fired. That wasn't ultimately important, but what was important was what would be moral and right? What would be honest? What would be God's way? Would it be right to erase the log of the experiment that caused the Pool Water to pulse and glow? It would be unlikely that anyone would stumble onto that particular combination of UV light at that wattage and frequency. Should she be deceptive for God? That's not what Jesus taught. "God, please guide me! I leave it in your control!"

Comforted by her prayer, Maria went back to sleep…

Chapter 15

MARIA'S MOTHER, ELZA, WAS IN the recreation room at Pleasant Acres checking her iPad, email, Facebook, and national news. All was flooded with the news, reactions, and commentary about the Pool of Siloam Apparition. She knew Maria would have some inside information about it, but she had not been able to reach her by phone or email.

Mr. Mosier left his card game and came to sit by Elza. "Waz up, Mama?" He said with his usual fun-loving inflection.

"Oh, Mr. Mosier, Have you heard about Jesus appearing at the Pool of Siloam?"

He said, "What? Whatever you're drinking, I want some too. Living Water?"

Elza smiled but said, "No, really! It's all over the news."

She began to update him on what had happened "...and so most people think it was a publicity stunt by the Israeli Government, but people that were there say it was Jesus without a doubt. They realize how their claim may look to most people, but they have been visibly affected. They don't seem to care if people don't believe them or think that they're crazy."

Mr. Mosier scoffed "Well, it's been said that Christ will return, but I would think that it would be for more than a minute. Interesting timing and location with the Pool of Siloam Water being talked about as it is. What does your daughter think about it?"

Elza shrugged, "I haven't been able to reach her. She was scheduled to be back from D.C yesterday, but she must be really busy. She hasn't returned my texts or phone calls."

"Jesus at the Pool of Siloam? Are you sure they're not putting something in your coffee?"

Elza laughed and said "No, they're not. I like my coffee like I like my men –very hot and black!"

At that Mr. Mosier was at a loss for words. He rolled his eyes, sighed and went to sit in an armchair nearby and look at a newspaper, which was full of news about the Pool of Siloam.

No more than a minute later he fell asleep in the chair. He began dreaming a reoccurring dream. He dreamed he was in a Mikvah surrounded by beautiful, love emitting, familiar strangers and a white-haired, white-robed, white-bearded man. Suddenly, the white-haired man dipped him backwards into the water which was neither cool nor warm. It was his exact body temperature. Under the water, he felt cleansed, with no stress, floating like a simple molecule of the Universe with no attachment except to a beam of unusual light beckoning from a distance…

Abruptly, the euphoric calm was interrupted, and fear and adrenaline invaded his mind. Mr. Mosier awakened to the sight of two third-world looking men trying to restrain Elza. She was screaming, "Help! Someone! Help!!"

Chapter 16

ABOUT 10 AM ANITA WELCOMED Maria to the lab. "Good morning, Maria. How are you? I see by the work log that you worked pretty late."

Maria's voice was a little deeper and sounded tired, as she said, "I did work pretty late, but I'm fine." In actuality she was tired but the coffee and excitement of it all was propelling her functionality.

"Anita, I think I found a break-through in a way to alter the Siloam Water. If it could be altered it might be possible to negate the negative effects."

Anita, having a keen scientific mind herself, began to calculate the impact of what Maria just told her. "Wow Maria, on one hand, if it could be altered and null the effects, it would prevent billions of humans of a certain ilk from dying if exposed. On the other hand, its healing powers could be lost to billions of other people.

What do we want to accomplish? Do we want to change it if we can? We actually have the apparent cure and prevention of cancer. But in achieving the cure, millions, if not billions, that will not open their eyes to see or, or …hear, or understand the Truth will be eradicated from the Earth!"

"Yes Anita, I thought all night about just what you are saying. I thought: What if we could alter it to just provide the benefits and not have the deadly negative side? But, I don't think that's God's Plan. I think God is displeased with the decisions of many of His people; to follow false god's, false doctrine, and evil paths that threaten his followers. I think these offenses have caused the end of God's loving patience and the elimination of the unbelievers is what is behind this supernatural phenomenon."

Anita replied, "God used water before to cleanse the Earth of unbelievers."

Maria continued, "Yes, I remembered that too, so I have decided that we must repeat and investigate the tests I did last night to see if we can see scientifically what was occurring."

"What results were you seeing?"

Maria answered. "At a UV frequency of 127 nanometers and a voltage of 300 watts, the water began to change. It was emitting an LED-type of light in a blueish/white color and vibrating. I could feel a personal physical change when it occurred as well. It was like an energy drain inside my body. I'll wear a bio-hazard suit next time we repeat the test."

"So, you're going to try to unravel this phenomenon that has obvious Divine purpose behind it?"

"I can't lie and deceive for God. It's our job at the company and our obedience to God to try to do what He teaches. He does not teach lying and deception."

"OK Maria, I understand. Let's see what we can discover."

"I will praise you, **LORD**.
 Although you were angry with me,
your anger has turned away
 and you have comforted me.
2 Surely God is my salvation;
 I will trust and not be afraid.
The **LORD**, the **LORD** himself, is my strength
and my defense; he has become my salvation."
3 With joy you will draw water
 from the wells of salvation

For the next 3 hours Maria and Anita retraced Maria's tests from the night before. They could not achieve any results. They followed the sequence fourteen times as documented on the lab log. They even looked at the security video. There was nothing unusual on the video – no glow, vibrating, or anything as Maria had described.

Baffled and slightly embarrassed Maria sighed, "Anita, I have never in my life seen something that was not there. There have been a lot of stressful events lately, and I was very tired, but I can't believe I was hallucinating. I'm going to go through the sequence one more time without the HazMat like last night."

For safety, Maria had Anita leave the room presumably to go to the vending and break area. Maria then went through the same sequence of irradiating the Water with the same sequence of the various UV frequencies as recorded on the log.

When she got to the step where she remembered the Water starting to glow and vibrate, it did not! However, concurrently, she heard a voice both inside her head and outside of her head say, "I AM THE LIVING WATER".

Maria gasped and said out loud, "Was that the voice

of Jesus, or do I need a psych evaluation?" After all that had recently occurred and been revealed, she leaned toward the first concept.

While hearing the voice, Maria experienced the opposite of the previous night's energy drain in her body. A stream of energy, excitement, adrenaline, and alertness flowed through her. She felt a compelling urge to go to the bathroom. She entered the private restroom in the lab. As she was preparing to go back into the lab, she heard Anita scream and the sound of a loud crash.

Maria opened the bathroom door to an alarming scene. Anita was lying bloody and motionless on the floor. Standing over her was a dark-featured man with a sharp object, possibly a knife or box cutter, in his hand. Maria quickly jumped back into the bathroom and locked the door.

Her heart was beating so fast her breathing couldn't keep up. She gasped for breath and tried to calm herself. Maria wasn't a brave person. When she saw a spider in her apartment she would hit it with a flat shoe 15 or 20 times-literally overkill. A large fly would have her running out of the apartment. It took her powerful intellect to create some "have to" faux bravery.

A hard pounding on the door started her fight or flight response again. Maria found it hard to breath.

"Winston, I know you are in there! Come out or I'll break down the door!"

Maria invested in some air and shouted "What do you want? Why are you here?"

In an agitated tone, he replied, "You know the information about the Weapon of Mass Destruction that your government is making to kill our people. You must give me all of the information about it. If you cooperate, I will let you live. If not, I will eliminate you because you are one of the most important scientists working on it. You must cooperate by giving me all of the data and information now, or we will kill your mother at her place for old people. We have taken capture of her there."

Chapter 17

CONCURRENTLY, AT PEACEFUL ACRES ASSISTED Living, the usual calm had been shattered by the two "Bad Guys" as assessed and labeled by Mr. Mosier. They had stabbed the orderly on duty, who was now unconscious in a pool of blood, and Elza was wrapped in a bear hug by one of the men.

As the other man was preparing duct tape with the obvious intent of wrapping it around Elza, Mr. Mosier (who wasn't really sure he wasn't dreaming) felt a package of emotion and adrenaline that included a loving, protective instinct; rage at all "Bad Guys"; action and adventure books he had read; His long-ago military training; his experience with the Hammer Throw in high school track; and his work experience at the ship yards in San Diego. At the ship yards Mr. Mosier would throw 20 or 25-pound sacks of grain or flour in a circular motion reminiscent of the technique he was taught to execute the Hammer Throw by his track coach.

All of these emotions, experiences, and a lifetime of maintaining top physical conditioning enabled his unexpected counter- attack on Elza's attackers in progress. Mr. Mosier quietly got out of the chair, grabbed the top of the adjacent pole lamp, swung it in that long-ago practiced motion, in perfect form, and crashed the heavy base into the right rear of the Tape-Man's skull as he was facing away from him. He fell hard to the floor and was motionless.

The second assailant, "Bad Guy Terrorist", as Mr. Mosier had now named him, who had his arms encompassing Elza, turned toward Mr. Mosier and drew his knife with obvious malice intended toward Mr. Mosier. Elza, now freed, could only think to throw her very hot, black coffee (as she likes it) on the back of the assailant's neck. Reactively, the man yelled and turned back toward her. This was all the opportunity Mr. Mosier needed. He still had part of the lamp in his hand. It had broken in two pieces with the impact to the Tape Man's skull. The exposed power cord was still attached. He wrapped one end around his right hand and threw the power cord lasso over the head and around the neck of the "Murderous, Nasty, Middle Eastern Villain". (now level 3 of Mr. Mosier's characterization of him).

He then put his knee into the assailant's back and pulled him backwards and down on top of Mr. Mosier resulting in both now being on the floor. This maneuver pulled him away from Elza and kept this "dumb, uneducated Son of a Bitch" (level 4) from being able to reach and do any harm to Mr. Mosier particularly on the right side as the knee held his body away out of reach.

Mr. Mosier held a death-grip on the cord digging into the adversaries' throat. "Satan's Minion" (level 5) struggled and even tried to cut the power cord from his neck with the knife, but it was so tight that he only cut his own neck with the attempt. He tried to wound Mr. Mosier in the upper-outer left thigh that could be reached by putting the knife in his left hand, however, his sequence of struggle and attempt to cut the choking power cord during life- threatening panic had resulted in his rapidly beating heart pulsing out blood from his neck at a high rate. He lost strength and then consciousness while attempting to move the knife into his left hand in an attempt to deter Mr. Mosier, who had the Bulldog-grip outstanding choking him in addition to the blood loss from his self-inflicted neck wound.

The nearby patients joined the attack. Some threw more hot coffee at the "Monster", burning his arms, neck, and face. One lady poured the half-filled coffee pot on his crotch saying "Show that to those ugly virgins!" Another woman ran up on his shin with her wheelchair. An old man gathered on the other side of her and came up and down on his other shin with his walker. Another big-boned woman poked him in the ribs with her cane. Another stuck him in the upper arm with a plastic fork.

The scene was similar to a Committee, (which is the proper name for a group of Vultures) attacking a dead animal in the wild. The proper name for a Committee feeding is a Wake.

The residents had all accumulated suffering in various degrees. They had a lifetime of frustration, disappointment, pain, and resentment. They had to deal mentally and physically with normal adversity plus the added measure of infirmities, anxieties, and losses associated with their respective age and genetics. The ability to release, as they were individually capable, this pent-up tension and revenge on this symbolic man of oppression and evil was cathartic (from the Greek word katharsis meaning purging or cleansing). It was a satisfying and justified, protective retaliation of the weak against threatening, strong evil.

Chapter 18

TRAPPED IN THE BATHROOM AT her lab at I.S.S. by the Man- with-The-Demonstrative–Proclivity-for-Killing, Maria used her computer-like brain to quickly formulate a sequence of possible survival option resources. Ideas flowed through her cerebral system at the speed of electricity to rapidly list and evaluate the best plan to optimize her response. Within a couple of seconds, she processed these thoughts (among others):

1. Maria's first thought of calling for help was not possible as she had left her phone on the charger in the lab.

2. There were no windows in the bathroom to exit from.

3. No one could hear her if she yelled out.

4. She had no MacGyver-like chemicals to combine into an explosive.

5. There was no electrical source to create a shock apparatus.

She looked in her purse, found car keys, and began to consider them as possible weapon. She knew that, by holding the key fob in her hand and extending the key out through her fingers, she could possibly puncture his eye, temple, or neck. She calculated the extended key of her Toyota Corolla to be about 2 inches in length.

She recalled a detailed memory of an anatomy book acquired at the flea market. One Sunday as she was riding with her parents, they came upon a small flea market. Her Dad decided to stop and look around. Maria was sixteen years old at the time. He told her that she could have anything she wanted if she found something she liked. Her only choice was an old anatomical book of illustrations of the human nervous system; probably used at one time at a medical school. She was fascinated with it and studied it for hours and hours – amazed at the complexity of the human body. It reinforced her belief that only God could create such an incredible creation-and no two were alike! Like snowflakes in their singularity, but vastly more complex with system after system to enable and support life, and physical and mental functions, of course.

She could use this anatomical knowledge to her advantage today. She knew exactly where the jugular vein was located in his neck. If she had a direct puncture with the 1.5 inch of the key, he would bleed out quickly. The quick look at him gave her the data needed. He was about 6-feet-tall and about 200 pounds. At that size and weight, he would take about three minutes to bleed out, but would become weaker as the blood left his body. She might be able to outrun him around the room. He would be able to attack her in the time it would take to try to open the exit door. A puncture of the eye wouldn't stop him, but might distract him enough to give her another chance to puncture his neck. She asserted herself to be brave and go down fighting if necessary.

In her purse she also had a sanitary famine napkin. This triggered thoughts of using his assumed belief system against him.

Bam, Bam, Bam! He had kicked the door hard. It held for the moment, but scared her.

"Ok, give me a minute, I have diarrhea!"

"Diarrhea?" he questioned.

"Yeah, I'm sick; my shit's like water and smells worse than you do, you stupid murdering pig!!"

Where did that come from? she thought. *Oh yeah, my Dad would have stood up to anyone that tried to intimidate him. His Alpha Male DNA that I share.*

But intellectually speaking, what effect would that kind of retort have on this adversary? Her father had been killed on that backroad for not dimming his headlights when provoked by the gang on an initiation run. Her mother had always told Maria, "Sometimes you must lose to win."

It had already been spoken, so hopefully she unnerved him and put him on guard for a strong woman not normally encountered in his culture. What else could she do to affect him psychologically?

He said he has my mother. I should not provoke him to uncontrollable anger, she thought. *I need to stay calm and calculated. Not let fear, anger, or emotion influence me if I will survive.*

Her thoughts continued down that path. The diarrhea lie is a purposeful ruse to diminish any thoughts he may have toward sexual assault.

That was the first instinctual step in a sequence of a hastily formulated plan to begin to use his belief system as his vulnerability. The strategy of psychology, although admittedly desperate, had the best percentage of success in her estimation. His flawed beliefs were his vulnerability and had been all of his life she mused.

She thought, *Desperate people do desperate things!*

She prayed, *God give me your supernatural strength, power, and protection. —Please guide me!*

She thought of the Bible verse that states "God will be a shield for those who trust in Him" and "Although I walk through the valley of the shadow of death ..."

Maria had read accounts of interrogation techniques that were used at the detention facility at Guantanamo on terrorists and Jihadists. Some of the intimidation, threatening, and interrogation methods use on the prisoners included throwing what they thought was menstrual blood on them. This made them "unholy" and unworthy according to their beliefs. The physiological impact on them made it one of the most powerful techniques to "break them".

Maria had the sanitary feminine napkin in her purse and another one with some blood on it in the trash that she had disposed of earlier. She also had a shaving razor in her purse; useful for any stubble that might arise on her body that needed smoothing. She found the razor and cut herself on her upper inner thigh. She used the ensuing blood flow to soak her white panties in the crotch area to replicate menstrual blood. She then cut herself on the opposite side and soaked the feminine napkin that she retrieved from the trash. She added as much blood as she could from the two cuts to a small cup that she ran a small amount of water in and then soaked the used napkin in it to make the water as red as possible and then withdrew it dripping red with blood/water.

This next step was the most difficult. She yelled, "Get back from the door and make some noise so I know where you are and I'll come out and talk to you!"

She then quickly disrobed except for her shoes and the bloody panties. The plan was to emerge from the bathroom naked except for the blood-soaked panties and dripping the menstrual blood from the sanitary napkin and hiding the key in her other hand. She knew that looking at a naked woman was against their strict religious teaching. That and the menstrual blood would probably unnerve him and give her a distraction so that she could improve her chances to use the key/weapon.

He said, "I am back in the room now. Come out and give me what I want!"

Saying nothing more, Maria opened and peeked around the door to locate him and make sure he was alone. He was about twenty feet away. She took a deep breath and came out of the bathroom.

Chapter 19

TORNADOES DO STRANGE AND UNPRE-DICTABLE things; sudden, surgical destruction – destroying some property and lives and miraculously sparing adjacent others.

Once, in Oklahoma, a tornado removed the entirety of a residential home except for the dining table which was still standing in what used to be the dining room. The owner's paycheck was all that was sitting on the dining table in the aftermath.

The powerful vacuum within the tornado spreads things apart and other things are trapped when the vacuum is removed by the exit of the tornado. Straw, paper, and cloth appear to be driven into trees; chickens are left in glass jars with narrow pouring spouts. An 80-foot billboard impaled by a 3,000-pound car is not an uncommon sight after a tornado.

An elderly man and his wife were running to a shelter from an approaching tornado. They were almost to the safety of the underground structure when the wife tripped and fell forward. The man looked back just as she was sand-blasted by the force of the tornadic winds. An hour later, they found only her skeleton; no clothes, skin, muscles, tendons, or shoes, only the weathered looking bones.

Seven days after the apparition at the Pool, a tornado descended, almost surgically, upon the pool of water where the appearance of the apparition of Jesus had appeared. It also occurred at the exact same time, as if organized by some event manager.

In addition to the often described "sound of a locomotive", there were booming cracks of thunder after temporarily blinding flashes of lightning. The sound intensity was such that if it had been able to be recorded without destroying the recording system, it would have taxed the best "Earthquake" speakers and sound systems in the best IMAX theaters. The film and audio would have been so terrifying that patrons would run from the theatre. Only the bravest and strongest could withstand the full experience.

It would be analogous to the electricity machines at arcades that challenge the operators to see how much electricity they can withstand as they squeeze the handle. The commercialization of the film of this supernatural event would be touted by: " See how many seconds you can withstand!"

How would film of Jesus's miracles have changed the course of history and mankind?

This powerful vacuum of the tornado inhaled the entirety of the existing water. It would be eventually replaced by the trickle from the Virgin Spring, but the entire pool and its contents was taken into the sky.

None of the security guards, staff, military or scientific personnel were harmed physically. Emotionally, mentally, and spiritually they were affected greatly. Most held such fear at being such close range to such an in-comprehensively powerful force that they immediately adopted life changing attitudes. The common consensus was the belief that it was a glimpse at God's power and concurrent surgical precision. The impact on their belief systems, life structure, and goals was dramatic; as was the cleansing of their lack of resistance to sinful nature. It was replaced by obedience.

Although no one there was killed, they were all doused with overspray of the water from the swirling wind. Soon after, only one person that was exposed to the Water began experiencing negative symptoms from the Pool of Siloam Syndrome. The rest began to be blessed with health improvements. Patience, kindness, and love grew exponentially daily for them as their emotional, physiological, and behavioral maladies of any consequence disappeared. If they did not believe in the Truth before the event, all but the one did afterward.

The Pool of Siloam Water wasn't contained any-more. Undoubtedly the Pool of Siloam Water would now dramatically accelerate its propagation globally...

Chapter 20

BOLDLY AND BRAVELY MARIA EXITED the small restroom within her lab at I.S.S. wearing only the white blood-soaked panties and her white lab shoes. She made a point to observe his reaction closely. He looked surprised but did not divert his eyes or look away.

She thought, *He's not that legalistic!* She quickly jumped back into the restroom and closed and locked the door. *That's a mental image for him to deal with. Maybe I can wear him down psychologically. He must be a religious fanatic or radical to be here doing what he is doing. I'm no match for him physically. My best chance for survival is a psychological battle.*

Maria couldn't help but to think of her Mother in danger, and Anita lying in blood on the lab floor. She set those thoughts aside and successfully focused on the immediate dangerous, possibly lethal, situation she was in.

He said in a loud mocking voice, "Winston, do you think I have not seen a naked woman before? Do you think I came all this way to rape a woman? I can do that in my home country whenever I want. Do you think we do not know about menstrual blood used in interrogations by your government? We are taught to avoid the blood for health reasons, but it isn't harmful, especially in Jihad or war situations. For a lead scientist, you are stupid and underestimate our intelligence. I'm not here for Jihad."

Maria asked, "Then why are you here and what do you want from me?"

She felt embarrassed and ashamed of her nakedness and her desperate ploy that was based on the typical stereotype. She was learning quickly and had to adjust her response.

He said, "I'm here to require you to give me the formula, the information, the antidote, and the preventative inoculation for the weapon of mass destruction your government is using on my people. You have poisoned my father, uncle and brother. My father has died of it, and my brother is nearly dead. I am here to get information to prevent the poison, to find a cure for those already poisoned and to revenge the killing of my family!"

As he spoke Maria put on her pants, top, and lab coat that was hanging in the restroom. The coat had a pocket at arm's length on both left and right sides where she could hide the car key that she could use to defend herself. She thought the lab coat made her look more professional and intellectual, which could be intimidating to him, if he saw her as an educated woman. She needed to try to recover from the naked faux pau.

She moved the conversation forward. "Ok, I'm coming out, but you don't want to kill me or my mother. I have the information to save your brother and your people, and you too. I have the preventive inoculation, and the antidote. Throw your knife on the floor where I can hear it fall, and I'll come out to give you what you want.

You have the life of my mother in your hands, but I have the life of your family, your people and even you in mine. I can tell you how they can be saved!"

He said, "Come out. I'll listen to what you have to say. I'm throwing down the knife."

She heard the sound of the knife hitting the floor. Maria said, "Sit down in the black chair. I'm coming out!"

As she moved into the lab, she took a closer look at him. He had the typical short, black hair, beard, and was probably late thirties. He was wearing a uniform of an IT company. She assumed that's how he got into the building. It was President's Day, so most employees were off that day. Anita had agreed to work that day and Sunday the previous day due to the urgency of the project and at Maria's request. What would you do on a day off if the world was at stake?

He was sitting in the black easy-chair as she had instructed him. She could see the knife on the floor about twelve feet from him. She felt encouraged that she had gained enough leverage to get him to comply. She noticed his eyes were dilated as if some drug was in his system. That could be dangerous, but it also could slow him down and impair his coordination in case of physical conflict.

She sat down about fifteen feet away from him and began the discourse.

"Sir, I think I understand your meaning, and I will give you the information you are seeking. However, let me say that this violence, and threats of killing will not accomplish anything for you."

Maria knew the authoritative tone could be pushing her luck, but she was testing it cautiously. "Let me confirm some possibilities to see if they line up with your experience. You say your father died. Was that recently?"

He nodded affirmative.

"And your brother is sick and has the same symptoms as your father?

He said, "Yes, and my uncle and many other people I know."

"Do they become dehydrated and their bones become weak and disintegrate? Do they smell bad like rotten eggs, but they aren't in any pain? No disrespect, but do they simulate a large, foul-smelling raisin?"

His face went dark, his eyes flashed with pain and anger at the memory, but he nodded yes.

"Ok Sir, I'll tell you the truth. That's all I can do. This will be difficult to believe, but it's the truth. I have recently given this same information to some high-profile government officials at the risk of losing my job due to its unbelievable nature, but it is true. We have been studying this for about eighteen months now. I can show you my written report for confirmation. This is killing some Americans too."

They both began to relax and not be so rigid. She noticed his tenseness diminishing.

Maria continued, "This is the basis of what you need to know. This is not some weapon created by our government, or any government. This is a disease created by God.

"Of course, all diseases are created by God, but this one is triggered and activated by drinking or being exposed to water from the relatively recently excavated Original Pool of Siloam in Jerusalem. This is the Pool that Jesus commanded the blind man to wash the clay mixture from his eyes that Jesus had placed. He obeyed and his sight was restored. The Pool has been covered for centuries, but recently discovered and restored by the Israeli government.

"Drinking or being exposed to this water from the Pool of Siloam triggers the onset of this condition, however, and this is the hard to believe part, if the person exposed doesn't truly believe in Jesus and God as his Heavenly Father, they contract the symptoms you have seen, and they die.

However, if they do truly believe in the doctrine of Jesus and God his Heavenly Father they have amazingly positive increases in health including cure of existing disease such as cancer, or any other disease or medical condition."

She paused to let him process the information.

He looked puzzled. "So, you are saying my father, and families are sick because they are not Christians!"

"Yes, we have studied this and know what the scientific things are that are going on, but we don't know exactly how the conclusion of the belief system is made by the disease. I know it's hard to believe. I'm an educated scientist, and I find it incredulous, but the facts have been checked many, many times. I know this is the truth."

He replied, "I think this is a cover story for this Weapon of Mass Destruction your government has created! And a stupid one at that! What proof do you have?"

Maria quickly said "No, no! To demonstrate and help my co-worker, let me get a sample of the Water from our vault and give some to her. May I do that? I think you will be convinced."

"Okay, but I am remembering that my father, uncle, and brother went from our home in Damascus to Jerusalem to catch a bus to Mecca for the annual pilgrimage. They stopped by the Pool of Siloam and got in the water up to their waist. It was after that trip to Mecca that they began to get sick. So, maybe you are telling me the truth. Maybe the Israelis created this bad water illness."

As he was remembering and telling his thoughts, Maria had moved to the vault and retrieved a small container that was labeled Pool of Siloam. He seemed to be starting to trust her and believe her.

She went to Anita, who Maria could tell was still breathing and poured some of the water in her open mouth. Anita didn't have any dramatic response, but Maria felt good that she had placed the healing water in her body. She knew Anita had the belief system to activate its healing and beneficial properties.

The Water was measured by I.S.S. and strictly accounted for. Maria had many times thought of taking some of it to her Mother to cure her health issues, but it wasn't legal, ethical, or literally, politically correct. It would have been grounds for being fired if she was caught and possibly would be prosecuted for theft of federal property. Maria thought in this emergency situation it was appropriate. She would take a chance on it helping Anita and being justified.

"Sir, our government has allocated a tremendous amount of money and resources, both personnel and equipment, to investigate this phenomenon. We would have been able to determine if the Israelis, or anyone, had altered, poisoned, or modified this Water. There is biblical history of the supernatural properties of the Pool of Siloam and its water.

"I have personally and professionally seen people with the same sickness you have seen change their belief system by accepting Jesus as the Son of the One and

Only God. If they are sincere, the sickness is reversed, and they are healed and are dramatically better than before the sickness began. This occurs with no medicine, no treatments, or therapy; Just faith in the true God and His Son, Jesus.

"I know it sounds miraculous, and it truly is. Jesus performed many documented miracles like healing, walking on water, feeding thousands with a few fish and loaves of bread. Jesus raised people from the dead and even arose from the dead Himself after being tortured and crucified. He said miracles were necessary to convince people to believe in his teachings.

"Jesus also warned that there would be many false prophets that would come after Him. If I give you logical reasons to believe in Jesus and His Father God, will you consider it? I am a scientist, not a religious professional, but I have proof that it can save your life and the lives of your people. That's what you really want, isn't it?"

Slightly agitated, he said, "Winston, you are a talker. I am confused now. I don't believe this Water can do what you say. I think it's a weapon you have developed! How could it do that? It's not possible for water to determine a person's thoughts about God!"

"I thought that, too, for many months. But just recently, with God's help, I determined how it works. "

She suddenly remembered details of a dream she had not remembered until that moment. "I had a dream that told me this, and I have started tests with one of my colleagues that is a neuroscientist. See if you can understand and follow me on what I am telling you. When a person is born, they have an undeveloped brain. At about twelve years old, their brain is about three pounds and is developed in size.

"When the person is taught information about Jesus or some other person of religion, there is a "marker" that develops in the brain. This "marker" is in the memory sections of the brain, which are connected to other sections of the brain that control complex functions such as breathing, sight, emotions, and psychological parameters.

"When taught the Truth about Jesus, this "marker" is developed in a way, that when exposed to the Pool of Siloam Water, it directs the brain to perform advanced healing and beneficial functions to the mind, body, and yes, soul.

"If the taught information is false, the "marker" is configured differently so that, if the water is absorbed, it directs the brain to perform negative activity, which soon causes a merciful death.

"This "marker" starts in the forebrain and extends all the way through to the cerebellum connecting all of the critical parts. It's a membrane that was thought to be just a structural support for the brain, but it is prepped for the catalyst which is the Pool of Siloam Water.

"This is exactly like the Seal of God on the forehead as spoken of in the Bible. It starts directly behind the forehead. The Bible states that the "Destroying Angel" will detect this Seal if the person is a believer and spare them from the Destroying Angel. In this case the "Destroying factor" is the Pool of Siloam Water.

"As I said, the marker is not developed enough until about twelve years old, the traditional age of accountability. We haven't seen a case of anyone under twelve years old with the symptoms – good or bad. Children must be taught the truth, or they will literally die when they get older and not go to be with God.

"You have seen people with the mark on their forehead; mostly ashes. This is symbolic and prophetic of what is happening now. It functions like the blood on the doorpost so the Angel of Death would Passover the household with the blood."

Maria didn't know she knew all this. She remembered even more detail coming to her from her dream the night before. She, in a sub-sleep state, had felt a sense of resolution and satisfaction, as if the puzzle was solved, but went back to sleep and didn't remember it until she started talking about it. Now hyper-alert because of the situation, she connected the dots as she was talking. That anatomy book she got at the flea market was committed to her memory as well as the bible verses, and her recent work examining the Pool of Siloam syndrome.

"So, you are saying that all I have to do is to get my brother and uncle to say they believe in Jesus and his Father God as the one true God and that the Bible is the truth and they will be healed?"

"No, they have to truly believe; not just say they do. It has to be in their heart, as we say, but actually in their brain. If they change their mind, it will change their MIND. Jesus gave a clue two thousand years ago. He said 'Love God with all your heart, with all your soul, and with all your MIND'. See Sir, if they change their mind, they will be saved."

"Let me see your report that you said you have for your government!" He seemed like he was getting angry, anxious, and impatient.

"Ok Sir, I have it in my files." She pointed to the file cabinets along the wall. As Maria walked to her file cabinet, he stood up and watched closely.

"Do not set off an alarm. I see your phone on the

charger. My phone isn't getting reception in here, but your mother is safe unless I call to tell them to kill her."

She nodded to acknowledge that she heard and understood him. She retrieved and handed him the report. It was bound in an official-looking binder.

She said, "I just presented this information at a high-level government meeting a few days ago. I wouldn't risk my job and reputation by giving them false information. I know it's difficult to believe. The government has made this a high priority. That means they're moving like a snail on steroids now."

He opened it and read the table of contents and glanced at some of the interior text. "I am taking this report. We have scientists too. Tell me more about this believing in Jesus."

Maria had been thinking in the couple of minutes while he was looking at the report. She was ready.

"Sir, there are many good things about your culture and obedience to what has been taught to you. In your culture the obedience is excellent. You obey the daily rituals of prayer at multiple times; you observe Ramadan, and follow common sense rules of cleanliness, healthy life style, and helping the poor. Most Christians are not as obedient or as active. Church on Sunday morning and a new Christian music CD on the front seat of their car many times is the extent of their obedience. Christians are educated beyond their obedience. Your culture is obedient beyond your education. This is true because you have been dramatically influenced by false prophets and peer pressure and intimidation by threats of punishment for not being obedient. But the problem is you don't believe in the actual *truth*.

"Jesus is the truth. In the bible it's written that Jesus

said I am the way, the *Truth*, and the Light. And whoever believes in Me will have eternal life. You and your people do not qualify." Maria paused for a deep breath. She prepared to confront him verbally.

"You, Sir, appear to be intelligent. That's a gift from God. In fact, you are God's idea, and he loves you as he does me." He got a reflective look to his face at that statement from her.

Encouraged by his response, Maria continued. "The fact that you speak English as well as your native language shows your intelligence – to be able to speak more than one language. Think about these things; the difference between your religion and what is taught by Jesus is one word- Love. Jesus loves you, and me, and all his creations – the people of the world. In demonstration of his love, Jesus endured torture, pain, and death to sacrifice for our sins and the failure of obedience.

"Jesus arose from the dead, lived on Earth again, and then ascended into heaven.There is no prophet other than Jesus that can demonstrate the supernatural ability to be able to overcome death. Jesus didn't die of an illness. He died a violent horrendous death and then miraculously came back to healthy life 3 days later and walked the Earth."

Maria's adversary said, "I have heard from our teachers that Jesus was a prophet but did not die. It was interrupted at the last moment. "

Maria asked "Then what were you taught happened to him?"

"He, uh, just ascended to Heaven."

Maria exclaimed "Well, that would be pretty supernatural! Use your intelligence to guide you to where to put your faith! Your prophet died of an illness and descended into a grave where his remains remain."

Maria was gaining some steam and her Alpha Male Father's influence again took over somewhat tempered with her mother's kind logic. "To help you see the truth and make the correct choice and be saved, use your mind and look at the comparative history. Your prophet's father died of illness before he was even born. His mother died of illness when he was 8 years old, leaving him an orphan. He was taken in by his uncle and learned to be a merchant and became a very good salesman.

"He agreed to marry a much older, wealthy woman. She eventually died of illness. He had no idea of being a prophet until he was 40 years old. He claimed to be visited by the Angel Gabriel not God himself. So, he claimed to be a messenger of a Messenger. Others that wrote or spoke of his teaching were, at most, messengers of the messenger of the Messenger. He kept getting verses for 20 years a little at a time. That's a lot of visits for a busy Angel, don't you think?

"Upon inspection, they seem to be personally connected to events in his personal life including war, killing, and violent acts, intimidation, and threats. He contradicted his instructions on which direction to pray from Jerusalem to Mecca, his own birthplace, saying he was originally mistaken. Where did the mistake come from; Gabriel or God? Did the prayers to Jerusalem miss the target and were wasted?"

Middle Eastern Guy, at first, seemed to be getting angry, but then gradually calmed as Maria continued to present the historical facts in a way he had not thought of before.

"It's a known fact that he had 13 wives, one of which was 13 years old. He died of an illness as did his mother, father, and first wife. He was not protected by Allah. He did not sacrifice anything. He did not die a Martyr which is another word for idiot. He just got sick and died, but he instructs others to kill themselves and innocent people. Is this the history and behavior you accept for someone to guide your faith, life, and to trust to your after-life?"

"He said that Jesus was a prophet too."

Maria replied, "That's the age-old salesman trick of name dropping and applied association of a prominent well –respected figure to gain personal credibility. He talked of Moses and Abraham too. Right?"

He nodded affirmative. Maria was wound up now; unloading on what she always thought was stupid, obviously false propaganda that was so illogical that it was laughable that anyone would believe it.

"And what about this 72 virgins thing? Obedient men will get 72 virgins in Paradise! Men will have an intact physical body, even if they explode themselves into thousands of pieces? And the virgins will have intact physical bodies, and will remain virgins even after sex, and the men will permanently be erect and a woman will only get one man, but she should be satisfied with that? Do you really believe that? Is that what you believe? Do you have faith in that teaching? Is that why you're here? You believe you'll get 72 virgins? And an eternal erection! What a horrible reward!!"

He hung his head in shame and said weakly, "I came to help my family"

"Let's compare Jesus' history. He was born of virgin birth to loving parents. He was proclaimed the Messiah at birth by Angels to multiple groups of people. He was teaching at the temple at 12 years old. He performed supernatural miracles which could only be of Divine nature-healing and helping people. He taught love and compassion, not killing. He never married, sinned, was ill, or hurt anyone. He accepted a horrible death to prove God's love, His love, and a divine gateway to forgiveness as a father would forgive his errant children. Miraculously, and Divinely he returned to life after being put to death, proving to all that opened their eyes to see that He was who he said – The Son of God and the Son of Man.

"Sir, I am a scientist, not a preacher or teacher. The choice is yours. I want my mother and myself to come to no harm, but I can only tell you the truth. This is what you came for. This information will save your loved ones and you too. I have no fear. If you kill me now I will join Jesus in God's Heaven. What would happen to you if you died now?

"I have a personal relationship with God. I can pray anytime, anywhere, and feel his presence. He is with me always. He is not a disciplinarian or a God to be feared if I do something wrong. He is a loving, caring, forgiving God that gently guides me and helps me to reach our ultimate goal which is to be with Him. What is your relationship with your Allah? Would you drink the water?"

"No, it's a poison!" he exclaimed.

"Only if your mind and belief system has been poisoned. I don't know if you know much about the Bible, but water has been a rich topic in so many ways. It's mentioned over 700 times. There have been clues and extensive meaning in the use. Jesus walked on water, was baptized in water and advocates cleansing baptism. He turned water to wine. He said 'I am the Living Water.' God parted the water for Moses. Jesus had the blind man wash his eyes in the Pool of Siloam; God cleansed the world with floods, saving only Noah and all on Noah's Ark. When Jesus was pierced on the cross, blood and water came from his side. Catholics sprinkle with Holy Water, Jesus washed the feet of the Disciples with water. How much evidence do you need to understand?"

Maria got her second wind and bore down. "Sir, as I said, I think that you have been deceived from birth. In your environment you have not been told the truth, so you haven't had the opportunity to make a personal decision. God grants us free will. He doesn't treat us like little action figures or toys or an ant farm if you know what I mean by that. He designed us to be very complex individuals but equipped with the ability to make our own decisions. You have just been told the truth by me. Now you can make the decision to follow the truth or not. If you make the wrong decision you will face death, but it is your decision.

"Believe the truth now, repent, and ask for forgiveness and your sins will be forgiven. Even if you spend the rest of your life in prison, you will spend eternity in Heaven if you sincerely believe in Jesus and God the Father. You will have the knowledge to save your family and people, even from prison. Walk out of here now, and I will only call EMS for her." Maria pointed at Anita. "I will not call the police. Take my report with you. I will do nothing but pray for you and your family. If you get captured, just pray and trust in Jesus as God's Son and you will be fine."

He looked somewhat subdued, and Maria could see him thinking hard about what she presented.

"You must act quickly. Just yesterday, Jesus appeared at the Pool of Siloam and said 'I am The Living Water. He that believes in Me will not perish but have Infinite Life."

Suddenly his eyes flashed and his pupils became black and large. "What do you take me for?" he shouted.

101

"I am no fool. Jesus didn't appear at the Pool of Siloam! I know you are lying now! I was starting to believe you."

Maria countered "No! He was warning those that would hear and listen to believe in Him. Look at your phone and check the news!" It's all over the news!"

"I told you that I can't get a signal here!! You're a liar!" He then produced another knife from his sleeve. His eyes appeared even more dilated. Maria knew that his hometown of Damascus was known for their craftsmanship of knives. She knew it would be deadly; overmatching her car key weapon. She reached into her pocket.

Chapter 21

HE SHOUTED SOMETHING IN ARABIC and advanced toward her. Maria turned and ran. She had a beaker of acid nearby and thought of grabbing it and throwing it at him. She located the car key in her pocket and put it in her hand protruding through her fingers as planned. Just as she was about to reach the beaker, he grabbed her from behind by her long, black hair. She turned just in time so see him start the knife in the direction of her ribs.

The knife was intercepted by wings. Maria instantly thought, *What? FEATHERS! Am I dead or hallucinating?*

Standing between her and her assailant was a 7-foot-tall creature with six wings, the face of a man facing forward, an eagle, an ox, and a lion facing in the other three directions. Heat was filling the area as well as smoke. An eerie sound vibrated her and the room. Maria recognized it as a Seraph that guarded the gate in the Garden of Eden and was seen by Isaiah and John in biblical descriptions. The Seraph encompassed Maria's attacker with two wings and began to hold him as if ready to take him away.

Maria was overcome with a powerful spirit. She had

never felt such a sensation. Instinctively she yelled, "Leave Him! In Jesus name! Leave him! In Jesus name leave him!"

The Seraph let go. It produced a red-hot coal and touched the burning rock to the lips of the man he had just released. He screamed as the coal burned. The Seraph disappeared in an instant.

The smoke detectors in the room went off causing an alarm to sound and the sprinklers to start flooding the room with water spray. Her assailant lay on the floor in traditional prayer position on his knees and head on the ground as the water covered him. He was weeping uncontrollably and saying, "I believe in Jesus! Forgive me! I believe in Jesus, Jesus, Jesus! Jesus!"

Maria said, "You were just saved by the name of Jesus!" He continued to sob.

The door to the lab was broken open at that moment. It was the police. They looked upon the scene with incredulous eyes.

Maria shouted, "My mother?!"

An officer said, "She's safe!"

Maria collapsed to the wet floor.

Genesis:
22 Then the LORD God said, "Behold, the man has become like one of Us, knowing good and evil; and now, he might stretch out his hand, and take also from the tree of life, and eat, and live forever"— 23 therefore the LORD God sent him out from the garden of Eden, to cultivate the ground from which he was taken. 24 So He drove the man out; and at the east of the garden of Eden He stationed the cherubim and the flaming sword which

104

turned every direction to guard the way to the tree of life.

Isaiah's Vision

6 In the year of King Uzziah's death I saw the Lord sitting on a throne, lofty and exalted, with the train of His robe filling the temple. 2 Seraphim stood above Him, each having six wings: with two he covered his face, and with two he covered his feet, and with two he flew. 3 And one called out to another and said,

"Holy, Holy, Holy, is the LORD of hosts,

The]whole earth is full of His glory."

4 And the foundations of the thresholds trembled at the voice of him who called out, while the] temple was filling with smoke. 5 Then I said,

"Woe is me, for I am ruined!

Because I am a man of unclean lips,

And I live among a people of unclean lips;

For my eyes have seen the King, the LORD of hosts."

6 Then one of the seraphim flew to me with a burning coal in his hand, which he had taken from the altar with tongs. 7 He touched my mouth *with it* and said, "Behold, this has touched your lips; and your iniquity is taken away and your sin is forgiven.

Chapter 22

MARIA WOKE UP IN A hospital bed. She was the only one there. She tried to focus on what happened and what was immediately happening. She noticed the IV in her arm. Her thoughts went to the events in the lab. She reviewed what she said and did, and the sequence of events. When she got to the intervention of the Seraph, she sat up quickly in the bed. Her eyes were wide. She thought, *Was the Seraph real or a hallucination? Was I being protected by God? Why me?*

Maria had more questions. She pushed the call button. A nurse came in about a minute.

The nurse said "Welcome back Ms. Hero!"

"Hero?"

The nurse replied, "Yes, you subdued a wanted terrorist that had been on the FBI list for some time. Everyone is talking about it. We've had to hide you from the news media. How are you feeling?"

Maria asked "How long have I been out?"

The nurse looked at her watch. "About 26 hours. How are you feeling?"

"I'm ok." She noticed some bruises, on her arms.

The nurse noticed her gaze and said, "You had some bruises and some cuts in your groin region. But otherwise you just were low on a lot of things including energy. We're giving you a boost with the IV. We'll get the Doctor here soon to check you."

"Where's my mother and my lab assistant Anita?"

"Your mother is at the retirement home, doing fine. There was a ruckus there that is being investigated. The police need her there to give reports, but she wanted to know about you as soon as you woke up."

Maria questioned, "Ruckus?"

"There was an attack there, but some 80 or 90-year-old guy took out two terrorists. He's being called a hero too."

Maria thought, *I wonder if there was some divine intervention there, too?*

She asked "And what about Anita, and what happened to MY terrorist?"

The nurse said, "Anita is in critical care, but is stable and is recovering amazingly well for someone that lost that much blood. Your terrorist is in custody and the police are very happy about that. Honey, you should rest, there are some people that want to talk to you after the Doctor says it's ok."

"People?"

"Yes, the Police, the FBI, your boss, and Anita's parents, and friends, and way too many people for now. You should continue to rest. I'll bring you some food." With that she left the room.

Maria laid on the bed and closed her eyes to remove any optic distractions, so she could continue to process in her mind the multitude of significant events and issues that seemed too overwhelming to comprehend.

She thought of the Pool of Siloam Syndrome and the scientific versus supernatural data; the report of the appearance and message of Jesus at the Pool of Siloam, the threat to her mother, the explanation of the way the Syndrome worked; the threat at the lab; but when her mind's logical, chronological sequence reached the Seraph, she had to stop the analysis. At that point she was overwhelmed and wasn't sure of her mental stability.

Maria prayed aloud, "God help me to understand. I leave it in your control. Thank you for your love and care and protection. Help me to comprehend what you reveal to me."

After the prayer Maria, still exhausted, fell asleep, but was awakened soon by the doctor.

After a short examination, the doctor cleared her for visitors. A delegation of authorities filled her small room and began to ask questions. Homeland Security, FBI, the Department of Justice, and the CDC wanted to know what happened.

Maria spoke of the events in sequence but before she got to the knife attack and intervention by the Seraph, she asked if they had looked at the security tape. They said yes, but it had stopped working for no known reason from the time she was conversing with the intruder until when the police came in the room. Maria realized that if there was no evidence of the Seraph, she would appear delusional, at the least, if she gave the information. She decided to say that she was not sure what happened and asked what they think happened.

The oldest, most official looking agent said that, apparently, the intruder had narcotics in his system and had a meltdown. The assailant claimed that a huge monster had attacked him and burned his lips. There were blisters on his lips and the sprinkler system had been triggered. They asked if maybe she threw some acid at him, causing the burns and smoky fumes to activate the sprinklers. She said the altercation had happened so quickly that it was kind of a blur, but she did remember running to a beaker of acid when he tried to attack her with a knife.

They said he keep repeating "Jesus" over and over.

When they finally left, Maria was exhausted. She called the nurse and asked for her phone. The nurse said it didn't arrive with her, so Maria turned on the television to relieve her mind for a few minutes of what she had experienced. Her mind wasn't relieved however. CNN was reporting something about the Pool of Siloam but went to commercial. Maria thought, *Oh what now!*

After the commercials the CNN report was presented about the tornado at the Pool of Siloam. They had interviews with people that were working there when it touched down and extracted the contents of the Pool. No one was killed, but the people interviewed were visibly unsettled and were in wondrous awe of the power and precision of the tornado, and thankful it didn't move 50 yards or so in their direction.

Maria spoke aloud, "The Water will now be propagated far and wide. The cleansing will advance rapidly." The process was becoming very clear to her.

She wondered about the power she felt to command the Seraph. Where did that come from?

Chapter 23

THE NEXT MORNING MARIA RECEIVED a call from Elza. Her mother told her in detail what occurred at the retirement center. Maria listening in amazement, but didn't tell her mother about the incident at the lab. Maria told her she would come to visit her soon and tell her the story.

Elza told Maria that they had Federal security there now, and she was safe but was looking forward to seeing her as soon as she could get there. Maria was feeling almost normal and had recovered with the rest and IV. It felt good talking to her mother.

The call was cut short when the President and CEO of I.S.S., Dr. Jacobs, came to visit with her in her hospital room. Dr. Jacobs said "Good morning Ms. Winston. How are you feeling?"

"Good morning, Dr. Jacobs, I feel fine this morning."

Dr. Jacobs said, "That's great. You look well. I came to check on you and congratulate you on a job well done in helping to catch the terrorist and protect Anita, and, of course yourself."

"Thank you, Sir."

Dr Jacobs said, "I've been given the reports and information about the incident and the corresponding attack on your mother at the retirement center. I also have been given your reports on your work with the Pool of Siloam Syndrome. Fascinating! This is an important project for I.S.S., and I want you to know that you have my full support with anything that you need to continue to move forward with your research and findings. Hopefully you will be able to be back to work soon. We very much appreciate you, and will compensate you for your valuable contributions."

Maria thought, *If I tell them about the Seraph, they will probably fire me, thinking I've lost my mind. Maybe I have?*

She replied, "Dr. Jacobs, thank you very much for your support and confidence. This is world–changing phenomena. I've discovered much more recently. I'm anxious to get back to work."

Dr. Jacobs said, "We have Federal security at I.S.S. now in addition to our private security. You'll be safe. We have security at your apartment, as well. If there is anything you need just let me know."

"Dr. Jacobs? There is one thing I'd like to ask. As you know, we have a small quantity of the Pool of Siloam Water. We measure it drop by drop and inventory it precisely. It is accounted for 100%. I would like to ask for a small amount so that I could give it to my mother. As you also know by my reports, there is a healing power contained in the Water. I think she could be healed of her medical problems by the power of this Water combined with her faith. I, of course, would never take any of the Water without your consent."

Dr. Jacobs said, "Yes Maria, you can take what you

need. Just keep an inventory. I hope it works as you think to help your mother."

"Oh, Dr. Jacobs, thank you so much!. I'll just take 100 ccs."

Maria was thrilled at the prospect of the benefits of the Water to her mother.

Chapter 24

SUNDAY HAD FINALLY ARRIVED. MARIA thought about skipping church but couldn't. She needed all of the spiritual reinforcement she could get. She had told her Mother that she would see her after church. It would the first time since the incidents, and Maria told Elza that she had a wonderful surprise for her.

In the trunk of her car, Maria had the 100ccs of The Pool of Siloam Water. After church and picking up her mother's favorite Chinese food take out, she headed to the retirement center.

About two miles into the drive, two things occurred. First, a man was attempting to cross the highway and was standing halfway in the center of the four lanes, Second, the car in the right lane next to Maria apparently didn't see Maria's car and started moving into her lane to pass a slow-moving car. Maria swerved to the left to keep the other car from hitting her from the side, but couldn't keep moving away, or she would run into the pedestrian in the middle of the four lanes.

Trapped, Maria hit the brakes hard to allow the in-truding car to get ahead and into her lane. Unfortunately, there was an 18-wheeler behind Maria that couldn't stop or swerve and it hit Maria's car square in the back. This spun Maria's car into the right side of the highway off of the pavement where it came to a halt in a cloud of dust and smoking tires. Maria was stunned but not hurt. Just as she got out of the car, leaking gasoline from the ruptured gas tank caught on fire and flames leapt from the back section of her car.

Maria screamed, "I have some Water in the trunk. I have some Water in the trunk!!"

The truck driver, now there to render assistance, grabbed Maria and pulled her away from the burning car. He said, "It's just water. Don't worry about it!"

As they moved about 50 feet away, the gas tank exploded, and it became a Toyota Fireball. Maria knew the Water was destroyed. She wanted so much to please her mother and also help her mother. Now, she had bumbled this once–in- a -lifetime opportunity to do both. She had spent her whole life trying to please her demanding mother. Now she would have to face her scorn and implied incompetence.

She wasn't strong enough to handle more stress. This was more disappointment than she could bear. Maria wept.

Chapter 25

IT TOOK ABOUT THREE HOURS to clear the wreck. First, the fire department, followed by the police, the emergency medical personnel and equipment, then the tow truck. Maria sat on the back of the ambulance and was checked by the EMS staff. Her vitals were perfect. She had no injuries at all. Even her neck was not hurt or sore. They all said she was very fortunate.

As she was waiting, the truck driver came over to her and said "Ma'am, I'm so sorry that I hit you. Here, I brought you some water that I had in the truck to replace what was in your trunk. You seemed concerned about it."

Maria couldn't help but chuckle and replied as she took the water. "Thank you. That's very nice. It wasn't your fault. I stopped right in front of you. I had my foot on the brake when you hit me. If anything, it was the car that tried to change lanes into me that started the chain reaction. I guess they are a long way off by now. I'm Maria."

He was about 6 foot 2 inches tall, handsome and seemed naturally warm, friendly, respectful and just nice.

He held out his hand and said, "I'm Joe. Nice to

meet you, even under these circumstances. EMS said that you're ok?"

"I'm blessed to be uninjured."

Joe said, "God was watching out for you."

Maria thought but didn't say, *If you only knew. In the last week, I have been nearly killed by the evilest person I can imagine and nearly killed by Joe; the nicest person I can imagine.*

She just replied, "You can say that again".

Joe said, "Ok, That." and smiled.

Maria thought, *And a sense of humor too.*

She felt a strong, compelling attraction to him.

She said, Joe, if I or my insurance company need any information from you, do you have a business card?"

"Yes, I do" He handed her a professionally printed business card.

Looking at the card, Maria asked, "You do construction?"

He said, "Yes, and drive trucks in-between jobs. I like them both, but I don't usually run into beautiful ladies doing construction."

Maria smiled at the compliment and the "run into" reference.

Joe said, "My truck's fine; do you need a ride somewhere?"

Maria replied, "Thank you, Joe, but the police are going to take me to the rental car agency. I already have a car reserved there. I need to get to my mother's. I've been out of town and she's anxious for me to get there."

"Well, once again, my apologies for running into you"

"No worries, Joe. It could have been much worse."

Joe nodded in agreement. "Like I said, God was watching out for you and me too!"

Chapter 26

A COUPLE OF HOURS LATER, MARIA arrived at the retirement center. There was an inordinate amount of security, but she finally was cleared and able to go to her Elza's room.

There was guard at the door of her room. Maria showed him her pass and he allowed her to enter.

"Mary!! Mary!" Elza exclaimed.

Maria was surprised. Elza's pet name for Maria was Mary. A contraction of Ma- ree – ah, Mar-ee was shorter, but Elza hadn't used it since Maria was a small child.

"Oh, I'm so glad to see you! We have a lot to talk about! I'm so glad you're safe." Elza said as they hugged each other.

"Yes Mom, I was so worried about you."

For the next few hours they talked and talked about what had happened. Maria had to leave out two things in her disclosures to her mother; The Seraphim and the Pool of Siloam Water that Maria was given by I.S.S. in response to her request to give some to her mother.

Maria knew her mother's faith would trigger the positive results of the Pool of Siloam Syndrome, but she felt like a failure for not getting the Water to her. She didn't want to tell her and risk having her mother be disappointed in her.

Elza finally asked. "You said you had a surprise for me?

Maria had to reply, "Yes Mom, I was bringing you some food from Houston's, your favorite, but it was burned up in my car when it caught on fire. I'm sorry."

"That's alright, Mary. I'm just glad you were not hurt."

Maria said, "Mom, it's nearly dark outside, how about a little walk outside before it gets too late?"

Elza answered excitedly. "Great, you walk, and I'll ride in my wheelchair!"

As they exited the building and moved around the beautifully landscaped grounds of the retirement center, Maria relaxed a little and began to enjoy being with her mom, her family. They were about a hundred yards away, nearly all the way to the back fence, when suddenly it began to rain hard.

It came straight down with no wind. It was warm and the water felt good in a comforting way. Just as Maria turned to head back to the Main Building, she heard two percussive metallic sounds. She looked down toward the direction of the sounds and saw two coins bouncing off of the walkway.

Maria picked them both up. As she looked at them her jaw dropped in disbelief. She recognized them as the same type of coins that were found imbedded in the plaster at the Pool of Siloam. They had the image of Alexander Jannaeus, the Ruler when the Pool of Siloam was built before Jesus was born. Maria remembered them from her research.

Maria had forgotten in all of the excitement, but suddenly remembered, the news report about the tornado at the Pool of Siloam. She had seen it on CNN a few days ago when she was in the hospital.

She thought, *This is incredible! These have to have been coins that were picked up by the tornado that occurred at the Pool. They traveled in the jet stream all the way to Texas and fell at my feet. This is another message from God!*

That means that this rain water is Pool of Siloam Water!

It's drenching my mother!

She is saved! Praise God!

She began to laugh and dance and emit little joyful screams of delight.

"Mother. You are saved! You are SAVED! YOU are saved! Thank God!! Praise God!

Maria was spinning Elza round and round in her wheelchair as they both became soaking wet in the glorious rainwater...

Epilogue

A S THE POOL OF SILOAM Water propagated vastly throughout the world, the effects were dramatic. As the obvious became known, People, who are mostly intelligent, began to turn away from the false beliefs, the charlatans, and the false prophets. The proof was shown to them, and they began to choose the life and afterlife redeeming Truth.

Economies changed. Religions changed, Temples, Mosques, Synagogues were converted and remodeled.

Industries changed. Medical and pharmaceutical companies had to re-invent themselves. They began promoting and selling calcium supplements to attempt to offset the hypocalcemia. These supplements only slowed the inevitable by a few weeks at most. In fact, combined with the dehydration caused by the Syndrome, which could not be slowed, the result was the tightened and dehydrated skin surrounding the bones creating the semblance of a shrink-wrapped skeleton.

Drinking more water didn't neutralize the condition. Non-Pool of Siloam water wasn't absorbed by the body, and Pool of Siloam water only intensified the adverse effects. The pharmaceutical companies experienced major management upheavals. Top level executives and owners gradually became extinct from The Cleansing.

Soon, there was not much demand for hospitals, doctors, or medical professionals. Only emergencies like accidents or car wrecks needed medical attention. Attorneys were not needed much. Police and military were severely reduced. Sin industries were decimated. Not that there was not sin. People are people with an inherent sinful nature re: The Garden of Eden; however, sin was greatly diminished.

New jobs were established. Major increases in organizations that purposely aided the poor or unfortunate created new employment; as did food production, housing, and transportation with "Green Earth" global initiatives.

There were no more religious conflicts. People believed in Jesus and God and The Holy Spirit or were erased so that the focus, the glorification, the Truth was magnified in the way it was intended. Muslims converted and brought with them their obedience and dedication and fervor. Christians were influenced in a positive way by this. The Truth with an increased measure of obedience, dedication, and enthusiasm, was a wonderful, awesome foundation for spiritual life.

After more research, Maria discovered that the Pool of Siloam Water, after being exposed to harmful pollutants existing around the world, had a half-life of about 20 years. After this amount of time, Mankind would begin to be on its own again.

Questionable decisions based on Free-will are probable to start to accumulate once again after this time. Lessons learned may, or may not, be forgotten.

Maria began a relationship with Joe. They made plans to get married. She told him, that she must remain a virgin until they were married. Joe, a strong Christian, agreed.

Upon encouragement from Elza, who was now living on her own in an apartment and doing well, Maria had the coins authenticated and appraised. She was offered $100,000 each for them. She said she didn't want to sell them.

After a routine blood test, Maria was called back in to the doctor.

The doctor told her she was pregnant. Maria said that was impossible, that she was a virgin. More tests confirmed that she was pregnant-and a virgin.

She had to tell Joe. He loved her so much by then, that he didn't even question her.

Joe had a dream that an Angel came to him and told him that he was not to worry.

It was confirmed that Maria's Baby was a Girl.

Another Virgin Birth? Incredible!

Maria did have indicators that she had been protected and had been given Divine information and then some kind of power over the Seraph. But just the presence of the Seraph was supernatural and having some power over it was beyond phenomenal.

She already was re-reading The Bible. After the experiences she had, the words jumped off of the page and had deeper meaning to her. Being exposed directly to what could only be called Supernatural and beyond science and natural order, the meaning and messages in the Bible had so much more dimension. It was as if the words were headlines and she could see the full meaning of the story.

Thinking about it, she thought she may have been tested when she thought she had discovered a way to alter the Water's effects and had to make the hard decision that would ultimately effect billions of people's lives. She chose what she knew that Jesus had taught. She couldn't lie for God. As it turned out, she couldn't replicate the experiment with the UV light, but nevertheless she had to make that extremely difficult decision. She remembered asking for God's help with the decision.

She began to suspect that she had been chosen, protected, and groomed to be the Mother of Jesus's Sister.

Maria thought *Maybe God wants to reveal more about His Deity, His Kingdom, and detail His love for Women as well as Men with a Sister of Jesus?*

The Sister of Jesus would continue God's ongoing revelations about Him through His Daughter. God's children can only comprehend a limited amount of Divine teaching at a time. Maybe after two thousand years it's time for God to reveal more?

4 For a thousand years in thy sight are but as yesterday when it is past, and as a watch in the night.

Maybe the Pool of Siloam Cleansing is God's way to protect Jesus's Sister from the result of 2 thousand years of sinful-natured people developing a spiritually toxic environment. Maybe God didn't want Her to be born into a world deficient in His Spiritual Plan.

Maria thought, *Were the coins not only a personal sign but financial support from God?*

Definitely the Earthly world is in the midst of dramatic change from the Pool of Siloam effects. IF I give birth to God's Daughter how will I, Joe, Mother, and the entire population be affected? How will my Child live Her life and be treated in modern times? What will She Teach? Will the things that happened to Jesus; the popularity; the persecution; the dying of a horrible death and rising from that to ascend to Her Heavenly Father, happen again in modern times? Will She perform Miracles?

There is no need for Her to sacrifice to atone for our sins. That has been accomplished by Jesus.

It's possible that she will be a teacher that will teach us more about God, especially about how women should be treated. She could guide the freedom of women that have been persecuted and abused by the false reli-

gions... Oh! imagine an internationally televised Bible Study with Her? She would be able to answer all of the accumulated questions over the last 2,000 years and correct the false interpretations.

What should I name Her?

Will I name Her or will God?

Have I already or will I come under spiritual attack? I have to protect this child with the help of God! What if She had been in the car seat in the back when the accident happened and Hell-fire engulfed the car?

Or am I just hormonal and imagining all of this? Is this just a mystery pregnancy? Did I somehow get pregnant with the encounter with the Seraph? ...

Maria's pregnant imagination was beginning to overwhelm. Then she thought: *I must leave it to God and -*

In about seven months I will start to find out!

Maria perceived this message:

> God loves His Son.
> God Loves His Daughter.
> God loves all of His Children.
> God is Love.
> Love is God...

Will <u>You</u> drink?